About the Author

Nicola Lindsay was born in London, and has lived abroad
for several years, travelling widely in Europe and America.
She says that she feels more of a sense of belonging and
purpose in Ireland than anywhere else in the world.

DIVING
THROUGH
CLOUDS

NICOLA LINDSAY

POOLBEG

Published 2001
by Poolbeg Press Ltd.
123 Grange Hill, Baldoyle,
Dublin 13, Ireland
Email: poolbeg@poolbeg.com
www.poolbeg.com

13 5 7 9 10 8 6 4 2

A catalogue record for this book is available from the British Library.

ISBN 1 84223 099 9

Cover Designed by Splash
Typeset by Patricia Hope in Goudy 11/14.5
Printed By Cox & Wyman

For Clemency Emmet and Anne McKenna
For their thoughtful criticism and affectionate support.

Acknowledgements

I would like to thank Paula Campbell of Poolbeg for the tremendous support, enthusiasm and effort she has put into the publication of this book. The mixture of professionalism and sense of humour she brings to the job has made her a great pleasure to work with.

Many thanks are due also to Gaye Shortland for her meticulous copy-editing, and to all the Poolbeg team involved who have been so helpful and pleasant.

And last but certainly not least, I would like to express appreciation of Kieran Devlin– a man among men – who told Paula that even he liked Diving through Clouds!

Navajo Poem

Do not stand at my grave and weep
I am not there, I do not sleep,
I am a thousand winds that blow
I am the diamond glints on snow
I am the sunlight on ripened grain
I am the gentle summer rain
When you awaken in the morning's hush
I am the swift uplifting rush
Of quiet birds in circled flight
I am the soft stars that shine at night.
Do not stand at my grave and cry.
I am not there. I did not die.

Chapter One

As far as they are concerned, I'm dead. But I'm not. Not quite! I'm still here, hovering above the hospital bed, trying to make up my mind if I should give up the ghost or slip back down there into that pathetic body of mine in the crumpled cotton nightdress.

As I hover, something, someone, tells me that I'd better make up my mind quickly. It's not really a difficult choice. Who's left to need me? Celia, our one and only daughter, stormed out of our lives eight long years ago, saying she never wanted to see either of us ever again. Amongst other things, she told us she'd rather die than go on pretending that everything was really all right and that we were a proper, 'normal' family.

I know there's no hope for William and me. Any feelings of love or tenderness we had for each other have been left behind, buried in the past.

I don't think I could stand any more hospital potions and proddings. They did their best but enough is enough.

So why am I hesitating? I suppose, if I'm honest, if I do let go I'm scared of what will happen next. Apart from wanting to be a nun after seeing Audrey Hepburn in *The Nun's Story* when I was sixteen, I never really had any religious leanings. If I'd been forced to make a choice, I would have opted for East rather than West when it came down to dogmas.

If I choose onwards and upwards, will it be all speeding along dark tunnels leading to an amazing light source with peace everlasting around the corner? Or will it mean just ceasing to be, nothingness, total oblivion? I think *that* possibility frightens me more than trying to explain the failures of a lifetime to serried ranks of angelic hosts. Perhaps they have some sort of heavenly tribunal where you confess your past misdemeanours. Now that we've managed to stumble this far into the new millennium, St Michael must be getting bored; he's heard it all before. A multitude of excuses for the inhumanity we humans dish out to each other.

A nurse is removing a vomit bowl and bloodstained paper towels from the bedside locker. The nice young doctor with the fair fuzzy hair and cold hands is writing down the time of death in his notes. My husband has moved to the side of the bed and is looking down at me, seemingly oblivious of the others' presence in the small room. He stands like this for several minutes without moving and then bends down and kisses me rather clumsily on the forehead. That comes as a bit of a surprise. William hasn't kissed me on the forehead – or anywhere else – for at least ten years. I catch a glimpse of his face as he slowly straightens himself and, for a moment, I think I see a look of real regret. Or am I just imagining things in my present half-present state?

The me down there is looking quite dreadful. My hair, what's left of it after the chemotherapy, is standing on end like an ageing punk rocker's and my face is all puffy and mottled. The combination of lung cancer and a congenitally dicky heart don't make for supermodel looks – more like something from *The Curse of the Mummy's Tomb* – that absurd film Celia and I watched all those years ago, huddled together on the sofa with our arms around the dog for his comforting warmth. In the really scary bits, Celia hid her face in his fur and refused to look.

William hasn't looked at me, I mean really looked at me, as though I were a person who merited attention, for longer than I care to remember. I hated the way he grew into being able to carry on as though I wasn't in the same room. I can't remember when it started but during these last few years, if I spoke, he'd look right through me as if I were a sheet of glass.

Not like in the early months of our marriage. Back then, his face used to light up when I took him a cup of coffee in his study lined with volumes of Knox, Luther, Aquinas, Teilhard de Chardin and François de Sales. He'd be working on his latest book, glasses perched on the end of his nose, hair all untidy from running his hands through it when he was stuck over something. I'd stand behind him at his desk and bury my face in the back of his neck, breathing him in, my arms around him. He used to like it when I did that – provided I didn't stay too long.

He used to call me his child-bride. A bit of an

exaggeration. I was twenty-five and he was only twelve years older. When I married William, I convinced myself that I was in love. I couldn't think straight; I was dizzy with admiration for his worldly knowledge and impressed to bits by all the books he'd written. I didn't realise then that I hadn't fallen in love with the man but with the idea of his cleverness. Perhaps unfairly, I expected him to be twelve years wiser in the ways of love. Foolish woman! I never knew when he'd experienced an orgasm because he never showed any signs of pleasure or abandonment. His love-making was always silent. It was as though he thought that to make any noise was the height of bad manners. So I learned to be silent too. After he turned away from me, I'd like awake in the dark, feeling strangely cheated and disappointed. After thirty-odd years of marriage I don't think there are any illusions left to be shattered. But I wish it hadn't ended like this, with the pair of us enemies sharing the same roof, so estranged that he hadn't liked visiting me in hospital. I knew that he didn't want to be there and he knew that I knew.

My husband turns from the bed abruptly as though he wants to leave, to get away as quickly as possible. He looks very drained as I watch him bend over to pick up his coat from the chair and then turn to speak to the young doctor. Seeing him so untypically defeated makes me suddenly sad. I know our marriage sometimes seemed like a gaol sentence but after years of misunderstandings and bitterness, I feel an unexpected surge of tenderness that takes me by surprise.

When it came down to it, I found the dying end of things

easy. The messy bit beforehand was hard to take, with all the bodily functions out of control and my brain and emotions decidedly off-kilter. It was distressing to watch myself decay bit by bit. I had the distinct impression that I'd started to resemble a hectically coloured Francis Bacon portrait with all the lines slightly blurred and my features slipping out of their correct position.

I tried hard to play the role of well-behaved patient, to pretend I didn't mind what was happening and that all the chemotherapy, vomiting and bloodletting were quite interesting when you got used to it. I pretended not to notice that my visitors were shocked by my appearance. I knew they were petrified of saying something inappropriate, that being in the same room with me made them worry about their own mortality. I also realised that they'd much rather be elsewhere. Most of them didn't stay very long and they tried their best to be quiet and sensitive. I wish I could say the same for Veronica.

Veronica and I have been friends since we were at school together. Most people would consider her to be my best friend. I suppose she is. We've certainly propped each other up, wept on one another's shoulders, fed each other Valium, strong gins and good advice on enough occasions. I just wish she'd learned to be a little less . . . dramatic. When I told her I'd been diagnosed as having cancer, she behaved very strangely. It was as if she was the one who was ill.

"Oh, my God!" she wailed. "What am I going to do? This is *so* unfair."

Then she burst into floods of tears and it was me who ended up feeding her Kleenex and trying to comfort her. Poor Veronica! Although she's fifty-four – the same age as me – she's never really grown up; never stopped acting out what she thought other people wanted her to be. When she meets someone new, she goes into frenetic overdrive. You can tell she's sizing them up, working out how best to woo them, to make them realise that she's just what was missing from their lives. Still, she's kind and very generous. After that first outburst of hers, I think she felt she'd rather blotted her copybook and she really did try to be supportive. She rang every day. Most days, she managed to get into the hospital to see me, bearing improbable gifts. Like the turquoise silk turban she'd bought in a brave attempt to stop me looking like a moulting hamster. She'd swoop into the room with armfuls of gardenias and orchids that quickly gave up trying to breathe in the overheated hospital air and shrivelled and died.

Veronica works for one of the largest casting agencies in Dublin and is always dashing around the place looking glamorous and slightly out of breath. She's tall and unforgivably slim. When *she* comes into a room, with her blue eyes and beautifully cut chestnut hair and expensive clothes, heads turn. They always have! I must admit though that after some of her visits, she left me feeling exhausted rather than comforted. Veronica talked, talks, in italics and exclamation marks.

"Kate! We've just landed the *biggest* contract," she'd exclaim, sitting down on the end of the bed with a thump, inadvertently crushing my feet under her.

"I've just got to tell you about this *gorgeous* young man I've found for the aftershave commercial. He's simply stunning!"

I'm surprised that she's made such a point of keeping in

touch over the years. Our lifestyles have been so very different. Me, buried in the Wicklow Mountains, content to garden and look after the house and get meals ready on time – and her, gadding around, still going to clubs and late-night parties like a woman half her age. You'd think she'd be just the sort of person who'd annoy William like mad but I've seen him looking at her sometimes with an amused expression, not irritated at all, as though he found all her good humour and daft excesses entertaining. I know perfectly well that if I'd started behaving like her, he'd have told me to stop being ridiculous.

Veronica won't miss me either – at least not for long. She's too busy to spend time grieving and I happen to know she's been planning a trip to Portugal. I saw the brochures sticking out of her bag last week. I'm glad she's going. She'll have a marvellous time; probably pick up some handsome younger man and come back all tanned and full of the joys of spring.

If I can't bring myself to go back then I have to go on, up, whatever. I'm not sure what I have to do to let the powers that be know I've made up my mind. Perhaps thinking it isn't enough. Perhaps I have to say it out loud so there's no doubt about it.

"I have decided I most definitely do *not* want to go back!"

There! No chance of that being misinterpreted.

It's funny – but I can't feel anything happening. I'm still hovering at roughly the same height, looking down on me, but now I've a sheet covering my face – which as far as I'm concerned is a vast improvement. That lot haven't wasted any time. If I were being critical, I'd say that they've been a touch hasty. They've definitely written me off as dead and no one is hanging around, waiting to see if I'm planning an encore.

I've suddenly remembered that Monty Python sketch. Will William demand a refund from the hospital because his wife is dead, is no more, will soon be pushing up daisies? He does so enjoy the adrenaline rush he gets from argument and litigation. On the other hand, it would be undignified and he dislikes situations that make it appear he's not in control.

Even though I've made up my mind to leave, I have a strange sensation of being tethered to the world below by a sort of invisible umbilical cord. I can't see why. Now that I jettisoned my body, I don't really have anything on which to attach an umbilical cord. I appear to me to exist as a vague, ectoplasmic shape, capable of mental activity, floating in space with nowhere to go and apparently nothing to do.

I also have the weirdest feeling that I'm being scrutinised by a Presence – with a capital P – somewhere close by. I don't feel threatened by it but I'm aware that I'm not up here on my own. I suppose I should find that a comforting thought.

It's now two hours since I officially died and nothing has bloody well happened! Up here, that is. Down below, they've been extremely efficient. My poor corpse has been washed – rather perfunctorily I thought. It's been rolled over and wads of brown cotton wool have been bunged into various orifices. I had to stop watching while they did that bit. It made my eyes start to water. They've even managed to give me some sort of a semblance of a hairstyle. However, I *don't* like the way they've tied a luggage label with my name on it around the big toe of my right foot. There must be a more tasteful way of keeping track of your corpses.

While the two nurses were tidying up what remained of me, they discussed their love lives in great detail. They – the love lives – seemed to consist of an awful lot of sighing over odd, very unlovable-sounding men. Though it's nice to know my death hasn't inhibited the march of romance. It was when they discussed their amorous adventures across the bed when I was still alive that it became a bit much to take. It's almost as though these young ones think that anyone over thirty hasn't got or doesn't want a love life. Anyone of *my* advanced years is well over the hill. If they only knew! I've had my moments.

If they only realised how much I've ached to be held lovingly during the past few years and, when it came for the time to die, to achieve that manoeuvre, not feeling I had to do it all on my own.

"She was a nice old thing," remarked Nurse Jenkins, pressing my eyelids firmly shut in a businesslike manner.

"Yeah, but I didn't fancy her other half. He looked a bit grim. Gave me the creeps the way he'd pretend he wasn't watching you and all the time you got the feeling he was criticising your every move. I caught him at it a couple of times." Nurse O'Halloran looked only mildly put out.

Observant young woman that! I'd noticed William doing it too.

The trolley came to cart me off to the morgue and they got

9

on with stripping the bed and chucking out some seriously sick chrysanthemums. Between them they polished off the box of Juicy Fruits Veronica left on her visit yesterday. She'd deposited it on the bedside locker with a wistful, almost guilty look, which I couldn't decipher. I hadn't got the energy to ask what she was thinking. She knew perfectly well I'd as much chance of munching my way through that lot as dancing a wild tango with one of the hospital porters. I suppose bringing things made her feel a bit better about the situation. I can't have been much fun during those last few visits.

I wonder where Veronica is at this moment.

Wow! And I mean Wow! I seem to have migrated halfway across Dublin. I suddenly find myself positioned, still hovering, above her smart apartment in Dublin 2. This is incredible! I had absolutely no feeling of travelling here. I just thought of Veronica, wondered what she was up to and here I am! No cancellations, no queuing, no no-leg room or being felled by someone's bottle of duty-free booze escaping from the hatch above during turbulence. This beats flying Aer Lingus any day!

She's lying on her satin-sheeted, king-size bed in her peach and cream bedroom, talking to someone on the phone. I can hear every word.

"Darling, I told you it wouldn't be long before it happened . . . Yes, I know how terrible these past few months have been for you, you poor lamb. . . I know, I know . . . but just think – now we can really be together."

I'm longing to find out what has happened and whom she can be together with. I can't quite tune into the other voice but I know it's male because Veronica's using her huskiest telephone voice. I seem to be getting some sort of interference. There's a mass of unsaid things floating around. Sometimes the spoken words and the still unspoken jostle against each other in the ether, making it very difficult to untangle what's being said. I am beginning to realise that I can occasionally hear her thoughts but it's rather like being at the end of multiple crossed lines. There's obviously a knack to all of this. No doubt I'll get the hang of it sooner or later. Perhaps I'm listening on the wrong frequency.

My name keeps cropping up.

"There's absolutely no need for you to feel guilty, my darling. You did everything you could for her and now it's time for you to be happy and enjoy your freedom. Kate would want it . . . I'm sure she would. Of course she cared about you, William. Kate would understand."

I can't help it but I've started jumping to some rather wild conclusions. For a moment, I feel in danger of dissolving – mental activity and all. In spite of myself, I have to go on listening, like a small child at the other side of a locked door.

"Why don't you come with me to Portugal? . . . Yes, I understand that you have to be careful . . . All right, William, if that's what you want. I'll go on my own after the funeral but don't forget, I've been patient for *ten* years. I so want to be with you, my darling."

Ten years! My God! I always suspected that William wandered from time to time – but with Veronica – and for the last ten years? It suddenly strikes me that she has been having an affair with my husband for one third of my married life.

I think of all the times I poured out my heart to her – and

11

I want to die with embarrassment. Though I realise that's not an option I have left to me.

I am so furious. If I had a body I'd be jumping up and down with white-hot rage. I haven't felt really angry for ages. For several years, all my emotions seemed to have become smothered under a sort of heavy blanket of making-do and pretence. Perhaps it's my anger that acts as rocket fuel because I suddenly find myself accelerating at the speed of light into the bedroom below. I come to an abrupt stop at the foot of the oversized bed.

I want desperately to *do* something: to show my anger, my hurt, my disappointment at my once-friend's betrayal. Her behaviour seems to me to be worse, much more dishonest, than William's. He gave up pretending that he loved me years ago.

I don't have a mouth to shout out words of rage and I don't have hands with which to shake her. I don't even have a foot at my disposal with which to kick her damned, squint-eyed Persian cat whom I have always loathed.

I, or what is left of me, float over to the chair where the animal is snoring on a velvet cushion. I wonder if I tried really hard, could I upset the little brute in some way? I focus on Zaza, concentrating all the energy left to me after a long and disabling illness.

To my surprise, the creature is suddenly wide awake – very wide awake. She stares, round-eyed, in my direction. The animal looks like a cartoon cat with all her fur standing on end. She's making the most extraordinary noise. It's a sort of cross between a moan and a snarl and it's full of rage and fright. Veronica's dropped the phone and is staring in amazement at her usually somnolent pet.

"Zaza! Whatever is it?"

Perhaps it's a good thing the animal can't talk. If it could, Veronica's own hair might be standing on end. Anyway, I've proof the cat knows I'm here. I wonder if I can attempt a little thought-transference. That's if there is any room in its brain for thought other than killing and food. I concentrate again.

It's exhausting but *infinitely* rewarding. One minute, Zaza is howling on her cushion; the next, she's catapulted herself across the room and sunk her efficient killer's claws into the white neck of the woman on the bed. I really hadn't meant her to go that far. Veronica too lets out a howl and leaps to her feet, frantically scrabbling at the crazed cat, who's clinging on for dear life, still letting off her banshee wails. Veronica finally beats her off by whacking her repeatedly with the nearest object – which happens to be a large bottle of eau de cologne. It shatters and Zaza drops to the carpet, bruised and drenched in a cloud of lavender. She hurtles out onto the balcony, fizzing and spitting like a cheap Chinese firework. She was lucky the doors weren't shut.

I can hear a voice demanding to know "what the hell is going on?" at the other end of the dropped phone.

Veronica's now collapsed back on to the edge of her bed looking stunned, breathing heavily and clutching her mangled throat. The air is heavy with the smell of lavender. I'm a little breathless myself. I'm also feeling rather ashamed – but I'm still so *angry* – and hurt.

13

Chapter Two

I've had time to get my breath back and I'm a little less furious now. I'm still hovering. I'm stationed over what was once my home. No, not a home in the true sense of the word. It is the house I lived in with William for all our married life.

I can see the roses badly need deadheading and the old apple-tree is smothered in fruit ready to be picked. The awful thing is, I can't *do* anything about sorting out the garden now. I know William will let it run wild. He was never interested in it. He said he liked nature left alone. It's already beginning to look a little uncared for. Not surprising when you think I was in hospital for the best part of three weeks and I hadn't been able to do much in the way of gardening for some time before that. If the young eucalyptus by the gate isn't staked before the autumn gales start, it'll come to grief. I know it will.

Three days have gone by since my departure from the world, although time in my dimension seems strangely elastic and I only know it's three days by listening to what people down there are saying.

William's been busy planning my funeral. He's spent ages on the phone with the undertaker. His book has been quite neglected since I left – died. He'd just begun to write a biography of the saint, Simeon Stylites. Apparently, he was an early Christian ascetic who spent most of his life perched on top of a pillar, preaching to the crowds. I suppose he felt safe up there. If he said anything too controversial, they couldn't get at him. Though he must have come down every now and then, when no one was looking, for a bite to eat and a trip to the loo. Typical of William to pick on someone like that to write about. I suspect there are often times when he wishes he could tell the world exactly what he thinks of it without anyone being in a position to answer back. Like some of the saints, my husband believes he is completely and utterly right.

I remember when Celia was quite small and very sweet and trusting. She'd just had her third birthday and had been given a box of brightly coloured felt-tipped pens. When she'd scribbled on all the available spare pieces of paper I'd given her, she climbed up onto the chair in her father's study. She covered every single page of a manuscript he'd just completed with circles and stabs of colour that went through the pages onto the ones below. When William came into the room, she showed him what she'd 'drawn' for him – delighted with her handiwork.

Silently and with a look of suffering, William had spanked her.

Afterwards, he insisted she be put in her bedroom. I

couldn't stand hearing the pathetic wailing from upstairs but William was adamant.

"She has to learn to respect other people's property," he said.

"But, William, she's only *three years old*, for God's sake."

"The earlier she learns, the better for everyone concerned."

"Celia thought she was doing something to please you. How could she know she was damaging your work?"

"She's an intelligent child and she'll be more careful in the future, Katherine. You can be sure of that."

He knew how much I disliked being called Katherine.

"But it's not right to spank a child that age. You could have explained quietly and gently. You could have made her understand, surely? Hitting her is not the right way to teach her. She doesn't know what she's done wrong," I blurted out, near to tears myself.

But I knew what *he* had just done was wrong, *so* wrong.

He stared at me as he often did – even then – with a look of barely contained impatience.

"What would you know? *I* have the welfare of our daughter and the entire family in mind in everything I do."

. . . And I did not?

Why didn't I realise there and then that I should just scoop Celia up in my arms and leave? I don't know where I would have gone but why didn't I have the strength of mind to act? Looking back at myself during those years of marriage to William, I can't help feeling that perhaps it's not surprising he trampled me under foot. I really was rather pathetic.

The odd thing is that now I'm feeling far from pathetic.

I would have thought that dying, if it didn't snuff you out completely, would tend to make you feel rather gently ethereal. Instead of which, I feel confused and . . . still rather vengeful. Being vengeful is not a nice trait. I'm not used to feeling like this and I don't much like it.

The Presence isn't any help. I know it's still there, keeping tabs on me, observing. I wonder, could it be some sort of a guardian angel? I may not have been very religious when I was alive but I always liked the idea that angels might exist. I sensed disapproval after my behaviour in Veronica's bedroom. When I regained hover-height, there was a distinctly frosty edge to the surrounding air that made me want to shiver.

William's found my Will, read it and rung our solicitor. Among other things, I'd mentioned to my husband that I wanted to be cremated; it's so much tidier doing it that way and there's something very sad about an uncared-for grave. He's told the solicitor that he wishes me to be buried. I wonder why? I thought William would have approved of cremation.

I've left more or less everything to William. Not that I had much to leave to anyone. I didn't have any money of my own and Celia won't get my personal things if she can't be found. I wonder if William will try and track her down, now that I'm gone. He wouldn't ever discuss it but I know he was terribly hurt by the things she said before she left.

I'd wanted Veronica to have the pretty opal ring my mother gave me when I was seventeen. I think that's not appropriate any longer but can I stop it? I do hope he's not thinking of giving her anything that was to have been

Celia's. What if our daughter decides to come home? Surely she will one day? No one could stay angry for ever. I know she once said she hated us both. What was it she screamed at me?

"I hate my father for being an arrogant bully and I hate you for not fighting him but most of all, I despise you for letting him walk all over you."

Celia was right. Of course I hadn't wanted it to happen but I had let him do just that.

She wasn't to know how good it had been with her father at the beginning and that our marriage had deteriorated bit by bit. She hadn't seen us together during that first year before I became pregnant.

I was happy then and I think William was too – in a sort of low-key way. He hadn't yet realised what a mistake he'd made by marrying me. Mind you, even then he wasn't exactly patient with me. I remember discovering the remains of a famine grave near the place they call *The Soldiers' Pool*. It struck me as such a desperately lonely, sad place. I couldn't get away quick enough. Later, when I tried to explain how I felt, William snorted and said I had an over-active imagination. In spite of that, we seemed to enjoy each other's company and when he'd finished his writing for the day, we went for long walks in the mountains, scrambling up through the forest to find where the hen harriers were nesting. He and I sat for hours, cushioned in the bracken, watching herds of deer move through the purple heather on the mountain opposite. We saw heron fishing the river below the house. On a couple of occasions we were spellbound by the sight of otters, playing on the sandy river bank near the rickety, wooden bridge. We lay in bed at night with the window opened so we could hear more clearly the sighing sound the wind made in the larches and the staccato bark of foxes.

I had always lived in Dublin and, at first, I found the strange night sounds alarming. William would take my arm and guide me along forest paths that seemed barely lit by a faint glimmer of starlight. It didn't matter how dark the night was; he never stumbled or tripped. It was as though he assumed that the path ahead was always well defined, whether going for a walk or planning his life.

Celia was eighteen when that final confrontation took place. She'd done badly in her exams and was refusing to repeat the last year at school.

"What's the point? I'm not academic. I don't want to go to university and end up writing boring tomes about religious freaks like you do," she shouted at her father, trying to wind him up.

"You don't have any choice in the matter, Celia," William replied, stonily unwound.

He didn't seem to care that laying down the law was like waving a red rag at a bull where Celia was concerned. From being a placid small child, she's grown into an impetuous girl with a fiery temper that used to alarm me.

"I've spent a lot of money on your education and it's not going to be wasted. You will repeat the year and this time you will work and you will improve your marks. You can forget about all that messing around with music lessons."

"I'm going to study the flute and you are not going to stop me."

"You will do as you are told."

19

"Or else? What, Daddy? Will you hit me again or lock me in my room? That won't work any more. I'm not afraid of you, even if *she* is."

The cold stare my daughter gave me was full of contempt. Even William looked taken aback by her manner. I watched them, holding my breath; the tall, dark-haired man and the stocky, freckled girl, facing each other across the kitchen table, both resolved not to give an inch. I wondered how could a once sweet-natured child have grown into this belligerent, determined young woman. But of course I knew how. If you bully and control someone for long enough, they will either back down, opting for the quiet life like I did or, at some point, they will turn on you.

"I'm not going to hang around here any longer. I've had it! I hate you both!" Her face was red and sweaty with anger as she banged the table with her fist. "I'm going away. If you won't help me do what's right for me, then I'll do it on my own – without your help."

· "If you leave, don't for one moment think we'll waste our time looking for you," said William.

Then he picked up some papers from the table and left the room without a backward glance. Again, I didn't *do* anything. I just let my eighteen-year-old daughter walk away down the drive in her pale blue jeans and her navy jacket. I remember thinking that her long, blonde hair could do with a wash. She was carrying her flute case and a small overnight bag was slung over her shoulder. I said to myself that was a good sign; that she'd be back when she'd let off some steam. She'd spend the night with one of her friends. It would all blow over. I thought that I would only make things worse if I tried to do anything – with the pair of them being so angry – and I didn't want to upset William any further. So I watched her go and said nothing.

I think the fact she said she despised me hurt more than her saying she hated me. I mean, people say they hate one another when really they love them very deeply and are just feeling angry or let down, don't they?

William has just told the local rector he wants me to be buried in the village churchyard. The notice has been organised for *The Irish Times* and apparently, my funeral will be held the day after tomorrow.

If I had ears, there would be steam pouring out of them. I'm trying hard to calm myself down but I feel so impotent. I never could think straight when I was really upset. William always kept deadly calm and logical during a confrontation, which used to make me even more frenziedly inarticulate than ever. I just want to know why he's doing this. I don't seem to be able to get inside his mind to hear what he's thinking. It's as though he uses some blocking technique to stop anyone from puzzling him out.

I do remember him once saying that Christians frowned on the custom of cremation because it interfered with their belief in the bodily resurrection of the dead. Judging from the state of my body last time I saw it, I'm quite happy for it not to be resurrected. I wouldn't mind one bit being re-incarnated looking like Kate Moss but I think that's highly unlikely.

I'm not sure I feel like attending this particular funeral. I suppose *she'll* be there with William.

21

Chapter Three

Two graves have been dug, ready for occupancy on the slope facing Glendalough. I don't know whom the other one is for. If you *have* to be buried, it's a beautiful place in which to rest. The mountain wind sweeps through the long grasses, and flying clouds decorate the mountainside in jagged jigsaw patterns of shadow and sun, making the heather suddenly glow like amethyst. The old yew trees stand guard like resolute sentries placed at regular intervals in the unkempt churchyard to keep an eye on the deceased. I should be content to have my bones laid here.

Unfortunately, I still can't get my mind around the fact that William has chosen to ignore my wishes. Any more than I can come to terms with his adultery with Veronica. It's not that I'm appalled at the thought of him having an affair. I'm the last person in the world in a position to criticise him for that. It's the fact that it was with her, my closest female friend – and that it went on for such a long time. When I think of all the deception their liaison must have involved over the years!

I have to give her credit though. She's looking pretty spectacular in black. Expensive black everything – from hat to shoes. Her legs are encased in the sheerest stockings (I know they're stockings, not tights, because she's worrying that one of her suspenders has come loose). I always envied Veronica her long legs and the fact that she has proper ankles. My legs were always short and ended abruptly in feet, with nothing resembling an ankle in between. In fact, her whole body shape is pretty perfect – even though she's not exactly in the first flush of youth; whereas I am or rather was, shaped a bit like a blancmange. A blancmange with unsatisfactory legs and no ankles.

She's standing beside William, lost in thought. Actually, her mind is in turmoil. She's made several attempts at some sort of short prayers – which surprises me. One part of her brain is trying to say a 'goodbye' and a half-hearted 'I'm sorry,' directed at me, I suppose. The other half is full of plans for how soon she can persuade William to move in with her – or she with him – after her holiday in Portugal.

I'm still finding it difficult to tune in to what my husband is thinking. I know he's uncomfortable, having to stand beside her. He's aroused by her closeness, her perfume, but at the same time acutely aware of the small group of my friends and various acquaintances, clustered around the grave. It shows in the little muscle tic under his left eye.

Half of the people here are covertly watching him to see how high he's measuring on the Richter scale of grief. The other half is wondering who Veronica is and whether she's destined to become wife number two. A group of my friends from the book club are here and I must admit that they *do* look upset. I notice they've been giving Veronica funny

23

looks as though they know she's up to no good. A lot of people, who might have come, aren't here – probably because the funeral was arranged at such short notice.

The ceremony's nearly over and my cardboard coffin is about to be lowered into the ground when Veronica catches my husband's eye and smiles a small, discreet smile. What she's thinking now doesn't match her demeanour one bit. She's thinking how much she wants to get him into bed with her and hoping people won't stay too long at the hotel tea and sandwiches do after this is all over.

Without really being able to help it, I find myself doing my sudden, accelerating bit again until I'm so close to them I can see where William cut himself on the side of his chin when shaving this morning.

"How *could* you?"

A sort of furious, invisible sigh erupts from me.

William suddenly puts his hand up to his neck and then nervously pretends to be smoothing down his hair. Veronica's reaction is more dramatic. She stiffens and then turns, eyes wide. I can hear her thinking, "What the hell was that?" I know she hasn't heard the words I used but she senses something is there and is unnerved. Good!

At that moment, they start to lower my coffin crookedly into that horrible, hungry hole in the earth. Veronica and William both take a step back and with one moment of pure concentration on my part, she slips on the plastic grass sheet that hides the mound of freshly dug soil. Suddenly, she finds herself losing her balance, falling backwards onto the green pseudo-turf behind her. As she falls, she clutches at William's arm. With a look of surprise, he staggers and then he too stumbles backwards, landing heavily on top of her. Veronica gives a gasp like a suddenly punctured tyre. There is a moment of startled silence and then helping hands hastily pull them to their feet.

When William fell, he somehow managed to knock against Veronica's hat, which is now sitting rather crookedly on her head – giving her the appearance of a rather tipsy Napoleon. One of her shoes has come off and there is a wide, very straight ladder running up the side of her stockinged leg. I can't help noticing that both she and William are quite muddy. Someone retrieves her shoe and, grim-faced, she jams it back on her foot, holding on to a tombstone with the other hand. Inwardly, she's swearing like a trooper and all thoughts of bed have faded from her mind – at least for the moment.

William has moved to a safe distance. He's seething at the indignity of being toppled by Veronica and knows the episode will be discussed and chuckled over in the village pub for weeks to come.

All of a sudden, instead of feeling smug at the sight of their discomfort, I feel like bursting into tears. I regain my former altitude.

As I suspected, The Presence is not amused. The temperature's dropped by at least ten degrees up here. I don't get a sensation of anger – just a kind of detached disapproval – perhaps disappointment? I can't see The Presence but I somehow know that if it wished to be seen, it would allow itself to become visible to me.

It's dark now and everyone has gone home. Even Veronica. William told her that he wanted to be on his own tonight and he would ring in a few days. She looked so disappointed, I almost felt sorry for the bloody woman.

He's sitting at the kitchen table, a glass of barely sipped whiskey in front of him. He's pale and I notice that he's developed a slight tremor in his hands, which rest on either side of the tumbler. There isn't a sound in the room and he hasn't bothered to light the fire. It feels cold and with only the one light on, uncosy. A Book of Common Prayer lies unopened beside him on the table. All the clutter I used to leave lying around: the bowl of fruit, my sewing box, seed catalogues, cookery books, all the domestic objects that make a place feel used, lived in, have been cleared away. In the few weeks that I was away in hospital, the room has taken on a male, sparse look. It reminds me of how the house was the first time I saw it when I'd just met William.

He'd shown me around, rather diffidently, as though wondering if what he was doing was wise, whether, later on, he would regret letting me see where and how he lived.

"You'll probably find this place rather uncomfortable after your parents' house."

"No, I think it's nice and the view from the windows is quite beautiful," I said, walking to the kitchen window and looking out.

Drifts of low cloud partly hid the rounded top of the mountain opposite. The river ran noisily over its stony bed at the bottom of the garden. Hazel catkins, like pale yellow caterpillars, hung from bare twigs. White stems of birches shone against the sere colours of winter bracken and the hollies glistened a shiny dark green after a sudden shower. A squirrel trapezed across trees at the other side of the river, its plume of a tail flowing behind it. After the dirt and fumes and noise of Dublin, it seemed like Heaven to me.

Then William turned me around to face him and we kissed for the first time, a gentle, chaste kiss that did not contain a trace of passion. It was as though, for him, it was a gesture of intent. I think he'd decided just then that he was tired of being lonely and had made up his mind to marry me.

He was so much taller than I was that I had to stand on tiptoe to kiss him. I thought he looked handsome, with his dark hair and eyes and lean face.

Later on, I suppose, I should have stopped to consider why a man who spent most of his time reading, writing and praying and who appeared to have no time for frivolity, should want to marry someone like me.

I'd spent the previous four years, living with my elderly parents and working as a modestly efficient medical secretary for an unpleasant, overbearing consultant in Dublin's Fitzwilliam Square. I read but not the sort of books that appealed to William. I loved going to the theatre. William did not. Every now and then, I would meet a small group of friends for a meal and some wine, to catch up on the gossip. Looking back, I believe he and I shared only one passion and that was for the Wicklow Mountains.

When I told Veronica, who'd met him only once, that I was thinking of marrying William, she was appalled.

"You *can't* go and bury yourself halfway up a mountain with that recluse."

"You've only been there in the rain. You should see it when the sun is shining and the place is smothered in bluebells and when the new lambs are skittering around. It's such a lovely, calm place to be. The air is so clean, I feel I'm breathing properly for the first time in my life when I'm up there."

"But you've only known the man for a few months, Kate. I agree there's something quite attractive about him but I don't know if he's right for you. You need someone who will make a fuss of you and make you laugh – like that nice French boyfriend you had."

"Oh, yes? You seem to have forgotten that after all the attention and presents I found out that 'my nice French boyfriend' had a nice girlfriend back in Paris – whom he has since married, by the way."

"OK! Bad example!" Veronica tried again. "What about that dishy new consultant at the clinic? He looks as though he could be fun!" Her blue eyes gleamed.

"Veronica! You know perfectly well that doctors are a no-no as far as I'm concerned. Especially the ones working at the clinic. The poor patients come at the bottom of their list of priorities. They're much too busy planning games of golf, ringing their stockbrokers and taking their smart wives and spoilt children to expensive health clubs. When they've lifted a few weights and swum a couple of lengths, then they're off to dine with the 'right' people."

Veronica looked at me in surprise.

"Goodness! You sound very savage all of a sudden. Not at all like the gentle Kate I know and love!"

"Yes, well, they make me *feel* savage. They're so arrogant and self-absorbed. They can be quite ruthless, you know, and most of their patients are nice, ordinary people who need a sympathetic ear and some good treatment. They don't get it and it makes me mad, that's all. It'll be so good to make a fresh start."

If I'm honest, even though I had agreed to marry William, I'd almost as many misgivings as Veronica had but I seemed to be hellbent on going ahead with my plans for 'a fresh start'. For some time, I'd been feeling as though I wasn't getting anywhere and I didn't have any real goals. I was just about the most un-ambitious person I knew but I did know that Veronica's life style was not for me. Anyway, she tactfully dropped the subject and I married William one sunny September morning when the world looked bright and warm and full of promise.

As I watch William now, sitting all alone at the kitchen table with the undrunk whiskey and the unopened prayer book, I remember how we never slept together before our marriage. I had wanted to but I think that perhaps he wanted to do things the right way – so that our marriage would start on the proper footing.

I realised after our daughter was born that William thought that sex with me had become distasteful. He used it as a weapon, knowing that I had needs that he either didn't have or had managed to smother. After an argument, I wanted to make abandoned love, to forget the harsh words and to start again. After each disagreement, William just withdrew into his writing and his prayers. I asked him once what it was he prayed for.

"For forgiveness, of course," he replied, irritated.

I wonder why he doesn't pray now. Wouldn't it be a comfort to him? I don't think he managed any prayers at the funeral – there was too much else going on.

I wonder too what it was that made him send a reluctant Veronica home on her own. He's looking so unhappy. I hadn't realised quite what a strange mix he is: one part all mortification of the flesh and turning away from life's pleasures; the other part, an ability to keep a clandestine affair under wraps for a decade, without apparently turning a hair.

He really shouldn't be here like this in a dark, cold house with no one for company. But I can't help being glad that she's not here tonight. If only there were some way of letting Celia know what's happened.

I know he's kept a photograph of her in the bottom drawer of his desk. He thought I didn't know about it. One day, when he'd left the drawer a little open, I found it when I was hoovering.

The door into his study is open now. I float my way over to the desk and open the drawer. When I say 'open the drawer,' I mean I *think* the drawer open. I make it slide to its limit and then watch as it lands on the floor with a crash. There's a moment's silence and then William appears in the doorway, looking alarmed. He immediately sees the spilled contents scattered on the carpet and nervously looks around the room. He walks over to the window, checks the catch and then turns back with a puzzled look. He starts to pick up folders and cheque books, finally coming across the photograph of his daughter.

It's a head-and-shoulders portrait one of her friends took during the summer holiday the year before she left us. She's smiling and at first glance seems happy enough but when you look closer, her eyes are guarded and the smile is composed rather than spontaneous. William glances at it and then almost throws it back into the drawer. He slams the drawer shut with such force that the sound vibrates unpleasantly through me.

How I wish I could materialise for a while and talk to him! I feel as though I would be able to grab his attention now in a way that I never could before. I know he thought I had nothing to say that was worth listening to but perhaps he would sit up and take notice of a ghostly image, swaying in the shadows, draped in diaphanous ectoplasm. I can just imagine myself in an elegant New Millennium version of *Blithe Spirit*.

I try thinking really hard about making an appearance, however amorphous, but all that happens is a feeling of pins and needles – so I give up the idea. I'm feeling quite tired – it's been a long day and it's debilitating, participating in one's own funeral. I drift over to where my husband is still kneeling on the floor and whisper Celia's name into his right ear with all the strength I have left.

William puts his hand up to his head – just like he did in the graveyard. Again, he scans the room for evidence of an intruder. Then he slowly gets up and walks back into the kitchen. I don't know what he heard, whether he heard anything. It strikes me that I really shouldn't be surprised. For years we've been switched off from each other when I was alive so why should I be able to tune into him successfully now that I am dead? I shall just have to find another way to get him to at least think about Celia, perhaps find some method of bringing them together.

I retreat from the room to my usual vantage point for a rest and a think. The temperature up here seems to have warmed a little, thank goodness.

Chapter Four

There's been rather a lot of time to think about things during the past few days. I've been trying to look back at my life objectively. That's not something one does very often when one is alive; you're busy getting on with the business of living and you're too close to people and events to stand back and be really objective.

I've been drawing up a list of good and bad points (just in case I do have to represent myself at some stage). I'm beginning to wonder if facing some sort of heavenly tribunal *is* a possibility after all. The instant nothingness-after-death theory has rather fallen by the wayside. From what I can make out, I'm in some sort of Limbo and I'm far from extinguished. I've no intention of going all pious though, like so many people do when thoughts of mortality occupy their minds because they're getting on a bit and they see their contemporaries keeling over, one by one. People who haven't been inside a church except for weddings and funerals, suddenly start devouring the family Bible as though they're cramming for finals. As far as I'm concerned, it's too late now for all that sort of carry-on.

The Presence is ever present and with a lot of effort on my part, we've been communicating in a limited way. I'm not very good at it yet. It's hard to send out only the thoughts you want to send. The other kind that I don't want anyone, least of all The Presence, to know about, keeps slipping through the net. Although I get the feeling he (I don't know why, but I can't help thinking of my angel as 'he') knows about even the ones I think I've successfully kept to myself. I've tried asking, 'What next? When will something happen that isn't self-generated?' If I'm reading him correctly, it seems that I've got a lot to do before I can progress to the next stage of my non-being.

Yesterday, I thought a lot about Milo. I should feel guilty about our affair – because, to be blunt, that's what it was – an affair. But when I think of Milo, I think of laughter and fun and feeling seventeen again – only happier.

I first saw him in the Co-op. I was dragging a giant bag of dog biscuits along one of the narrow aisles, lined with wellington boots and grass rakes and tins of weed killer.

"Here, let me do that!" he said, suddenly materialising out of nowhere.

"Oh, it's OK, thanks. I can manage."

"But I'd like to," he said simply, with a wide smile.

He was so tall! I looked up at his pleasant, sunburned face with its blue eyes. He seemed to radiate a sense of wellbeing and I thought how wholesome he looked – and how young. I let him take the bag. He hoisted it onto his shoulder as though it were a sack of feathers. I let him carry it out to the car and stow it into the boot. I think I started to fall for him right there and then. I know I was flattered that a slim, handsome man, who looked about twenty-five and young enough to be my son, had taken the trouble to help.

"You live at the other end of the village, don't you?" he said, after I'd thanked him.

He had his hand on the open door, making it awkward for me to get into the car without brushing past him and seeming rude.

"I do." I hesitated, intrigued as to why he should want to linger. "My husband and I have lived there for years."

He ignored the hint about my having a husband and gave me another wide grin.

"I've seen you working in your garden from the hill opposite. My name's Milo, by the way." He held out a hand.

"Kate Fitzgerald."

He held my hand briefly in a firm, warm grip and looked me straight in the eyes. I pulled away but not before a tingling feeling had shot up my arm and right through me. Uncomfortably aware that I had on my oldest and most shapeless trousers, that my shirt was sweaty and sticking to me and that I wasn't wearing a bra, I blushed, suddenly feeling ridiculous. I was behaving like a sixteen-year-old, not a married woman of forty-six.

"Well, it was nice to meet you, Milo. I must be on my way," I said, in my most businesslike manner.

He stepped back from the car, still watching me. I stalled the engine and was in such a hurry to get away that I nearly mowed down a couple of Wicklow farmers, deep in discussion beside some cattle troughs.

I looked in my rear-view mirror as I made it to the first bend. He was standing at the side of the road, watching. So were the farmers.

After that, everywhere I went, I seemed to fall over him. I found out that he was a student, working during his summer holidays, doing odd jobs on the surrounding farms and in people's gardens.

About a week after our first meeting, I'd just come out of the village post office when he drove up in a battered Renault with its aerial bent and front mudguard coming loose at one side. He stuck his head through the sliding window.

"Hi, Kate! Want a lift?"

"No, thanks. I enjoy walking when it's like this. You have to make the most of it up here in the mountains. One never knows how many days of summer weather we'll get."

The car door groaned as he opened it and climbed out. Again, I was struck by his height. He must have been well over six feet tall. Thick, curly black hair was blown back from his forehead by the warm summer wind. He had a young man's slender waist and hips and his jeans were moulded to strong, slim thighs. A green cotton T-shirt stretched over wide shoulders. I tried to think straight and say something politely mundane but all I could think of was how glorious he must look without any clothes on.

I became aware that he was watching me looking at him. I started to blush again. Until I bumped into Milo, I hadn't blushed for twenty years or more and it annoyed me that I wasn't in control of my emotions. Hurriedly, I said the first thing that came into my mind.

"I hear you're doing gardening jobs. We need some bracken and gorse clearing away on the hillside above the house. Would you be . . . available . . . to do some work?"

"No problem! When would you like me to start? I haven't got anything arranged for the next couple of days. I could come up this afternoon, if you like."

"Fine," I said. "See you at two o' clock then."

Appalled at what I had just done and doing my best to walk away up the dusty road in a nonchalant manner, I took myself to task. 'What on earth are you thinking of, Kate? You know perfectly well you'd decided to leave the gorse and bracken in the old paddock. Why play with fire? You idiot!'

I knew then that we would make love but I pushed it to the back of my mind and tried to pretend that after he'd cleared the paddock he would go away and I would carry on with my life as before. I didn't know that I had already begun to suffer from a sweet sickness that would turn me into a woman I never knew existed and that would make me incapable of making anything resembling an intelligent decision for some time.

William was away for a six-week lecture tour in the States and I'd been enjoying having the house to myself; indulging in things which he wouldn't have approved of. Like eating breakfast in bed with yesterday's paper and the dog spread-eagled happily over my feet, not tidying up the kitchen at the end of the day, sometimes not bothering to make the bed when I got up in the mornings. I enjoyed myself by experimenting with the hottest, spiciest, garlic-loaded curries that had the effect of making me jet-propelled for days afterwards. I moved the little telly from the kitchen onto the chest of drawers in our bedroom and watched slightly blue, very bad, late-night movies. I lay in bed and licked ice cream off a soup spoon, straight from the container like they do in American films.

I'd been feeling down for months. Celia had left six months before and, apart from a rather vague phone call from somewhere in France, telling me that she was fine and singing and playing the flute in a group, we had heard nothing from her. She hadn't wanted to talk to her father.

William had forbidden me to try and find her. I wouldn't have known where to start but I found his apparent total disinterest in his daughter's wellbeing chilling.

"You never learn, do you, Katherine? If she wants to cut herself off from us, that is her decision. Why make yourself miserable by going on a wild goose-chase when she doesn't want to be found? If you *did* find her, you wouldn't be able to make her come home if she didn't want to."

"But I miss her so much and I worry that she'll get into some sort of trouble. I just think that if I could talk to her, face to face, I would be able to persuade her to try again, give us another chance."

"It's not we who should be given another chance!" he almost shouted, "She's the one at fault, not us."

I was going to say that I didn't agree – that all three of us had made mistakes but William ended the discussion by walking out of the room, looking furious.

I was planning to commit adultery. I watched from the study window as Milo, stripped to the waist, hacked and dug and chopped. I tried doing things in the house but merely succeeded in stabbing myself on the hand with a kitchen knife. I wandered outside to try a little weeding in the vegetable garden but it was too hot. I picked up a book. It was no good! Each time I attempted to settle to a task, I would find myself staring vacantly into the distance, thinking of the young man working outside. I felt just as though I had drunk too much champagne: light-headed, foolish and very randy.

Milo worked all that afternoon without stopping. At six, I couldn't stand the feeling of physical and emotional tension any longer. It was as if I were an overstretched piece of elastic, ready to break with a resounding 'ping'. I was starting to wonder if I shouldn't just get in the car and drive off and not come back until it was dark. I didn't of course. I went out to the back terrace and called him.

"There's a cold drink in the kitchen if you'd like it."

My voice sounded odd. He straightened himself, easing his shoulders as he looked down at me.

"OK! I'll just finish digging this root out and I'll be down."

I went back into the house and sat at the table, waiting. I put my hands in my lap and made myself sit still. I tried to empty my mind of the man who would soon be stepping into my kitchen. I made a futile attempt at thinking of William. He hardly ever rang when he was away on one of his tours, so I wasn't even sure of his whereabouts.

There was the sound of footsteps and Milo's shadow moved on the wall opposite as he passed the window. The low evening sun shone through the open back door and he was silhouetted as he stood on the threshold.

"May I come in?"

"Yes, please. Come in."

My voice still sounded strange to my ears. I wondered if he noticed it too. I got up from the table clumsily and gestured over to the sink. "There's soap and a towel over there. Would you like a beer?"

"That would be great. Thanks."

I went and got two cans from the fridge and sat down again. Then I realised I hadn't put any glasses out. I got up and fetched a couple from the dresser and filled them with the cold beer.

Milo glanced around the kitchen as he dried his hands. "This is a nice room."

His eyes took in all the uncleared clutter I'd left lying on the table and on the decrepit sofa by the fireplace, old Samson (son of my much-loved labrador, Sam), lying in his dog basket, snoozing. Minerva, the moulting parrot that I had rescued from a bankrupt zoo, swinging thoughtfully on her perch repeatedly muttering, "Who rattled *his* cage?"

He picked up his glass of beer and downed it in three or four gulps. Then he walked over to where I sat, suddenly turned to jelly, wishing I was a hundred miles away.

He held out his hands and I found myself standing up and moving towards him, dizzy with anticipation. I can't remember how it happened or what I was thinking, if I *was* thinking, but the next thing I knew, he was kissing me and I him – quick, frantic kisses on lips and eyelids, on neck and forehead. I didn't try to stop him opening the buttons on my shirt or from sliding his hands inside. They were cool and smelled of soap and were slightly rough from the outside work he'd been doing. I remember, as he held my breasts,

39

that my whole body ached for him. More than anything in the world, I wanted to feel him moving inside me, to be filled with him.

"Which room?" he asked.

Silently, I led him to the spare bedroom thinking, 'I can't believe I'm doing this,' at the same time knowing that nothing on earth would stop me now. Milo started to pull off my shirt. His whole body smelt of sweat and sex. His hands were shaking. I experienced a brief moment of panic. This wasn't going to be like *Shirley Valentine*, with the man uncovering the older woman and passionately kissing her stretch marks because he said they were beautiful and she was beautiful. I didn't have stretch marks but I knew I wasn't the slightest bit beautiful. What would he think when he saw me naked?

As it turned out, Milo didn't seem the slightest bit taken aback by my full-bodied look. He didn't say he thought I was beautiful but he made love to me in a way that William had never done. I had never been so *intimate* with a man. He kissed me all over, even my feet, which I'd always thought of as ugly. For the first time in my life, I made love not worrying about doing something wrong or being maladroit. I licked and stroked and sucked and nibbled. For the first time ever, when I came, I cried out so loudly that Samson thought I was being attacked and started to bark in the next room. Everything we did together that afternoon felt perfectly and absolutely right.

Afterwards, we shared a bath and wallowed up to our chins in perfumed bubbles. I'd never had a bath with William. He would have snorted at the very idea of bubbles.

It was a tight squeeze and Milo burned himself on the hot tap but we laughed a lot. I realised I hadn't laughed for a long, long time.

That is what I remember most about Milo – laughter – and his sense of fun, that life was to be lived to the full and it was your fault if you didn't make the most of it while you had the chance.

"You've got bubbles on the end of your nose, Missus," he said, leaning forward to rub them off with his finger.

"I've bubbles in places I don't think bubbles should be," I said, giggling like a silly schoolgirl.

"Just show me where those bubbles are and I'll get rid of them for you."

And I did – and he did.

Afterwards, we slept and then I watched him as he dressed. He wasn't at all self-conscious when he was naked. He moved around the room in an unhurried, relaxed way – completely at home with himself and with the situation. I lay back on the pillows, satiated, and watched him. I loved the way the dark hair curled in a line down his belly towards his prick, the muscular smoothness of his buttocks and the way his whole body seemed so perfectly in proportion.

When he'd finished dressing, he said, "Do you want me to stay?"

"Yes, but I don't think you should."

"That's not what I asked." He smiled at me. "I want to know what you'd like me to do," he said, sitting on the edge of the bed and taking hold of my hand.

"I want us to make love again but I know that's not being sensible. I want us to find somewhere to make love that

41

isn't here. I know that I don't want you to stay the night because it would make me even more guilty than I know I'm going to feel when this is all over. I'm so happy just now that I haven't started to feel any guilt."

"Kate! Why are you talking about the end when we've only just begun?"

"Because, in four weeks' time, my husband will come home and when he does, I have to be in a fit state to welcome him back and to carry on."

"Why do you have to 'carry on' if it's not making you happy?"

"Because, my love, that's what married people do. They try to make the best out of a bad deal. They have to learn to live with their mistakes."

Milo looked at me, suddenly serious.

"Well, all I can say is, I hope if I ever get married my wife won't think of me as a mistake – and if she does – then I hope she will chuck me out and not pretend."

"I think any woman who marries you will be a very lucky woman indeed," I said – and I meant it.

We did find somewhere else where we could be together; a ruined stone cottage with half a roof, hidden by brambles and nettles – a poignant reminder of the famine times. We were lucky, no one ever disturbed us there and the days flowed by, untypically sunny and hot for early September in Ireland.

One week before William's return, we made love for the last time on Milo's sleeping bag under the birch trees behind the cottage. He had not wanted this to be our final meeting.

"Please, Milo. You have to do this for me or I won't be able to cope. I must have a full week to gather myself together again."

"Sounds like bloody Humpty Dumpty," he said, uncharacteristically grumpy.

"I *feel* a bit like him." I held his face between my hands. "We both know how lovely this time together has been. I'm going to do my best to not sour the memory of it by regrets or guilt. But I need this week to myself, to remember and to store it away in a safe part of my mind where it will do no harm to my husband. It's important that you understand."

There was a long silence. Then he put his arms around me.

"I will go because you ask me to but I don't want to. I don't understand why you feel you have to go back to a life that doesn't make you happy. I'll never understand that but I promise you, Kate, I won't ever forget either."

We made love for the last time and then we said our goodbyes and went our separate ways. He back to Dublin and me back to the house where Samson staggered to his feet, wagging welcomingly. Minerva just stuck her head out of her cage and said, "Bugger," twice, in a piercing voice.

I never saw Milo again.

I've tried asking The Presence if my affair with Milo might prove to be a problem but he was strangely unresponsive. He's still there though. I just get the feeling he's biding his time.

Chapter Five

I remember that William was in a dreadful mood when he returned from his lecture tour. I didn't mind really. I suppose, in a way, trying to please him, cheer him up, was like an act of reparation. He didn't say what was wrong; just seemed to withdraw into himself even more than before. I would find him standing by a window, looking out at nothing in particular with a troubled expression.

Two days after getting back, he dropped a bombshell during breakfast.

"I think it would be better if I moved my things into the spare bedroom," he said, almost casually.

"Why?"

I was dumbfounded. The thought crossed my mind that Milo had left some clue behind or that someone in the village had said something. Had our love-making been overheard?

"No particular reason," he replied, staring into his coffee with a bleak look. "I'm not sleeping too well at the moment and I don't want to disturb you."

"William, you spend so much of your time away from me: with the tours, your work at Trinity and in your study. I'm afraid that if we sleep apart, we won't ever see each other."

He gave a small laugh.

"I don't think you'll miss me much when you're asleep. You don't have to look so upset. It's just for the moment, that's all."

Before I could say anything more, he had done his getting-up-and-walking-out-of-the-room routine that always put paid to any further discussion.

The hot September weather ended in days of fine, drizzling rain when the tops of the mountains on the other side of the valley wore grey turbans of low cloud. William seemed to be absent from home more than usual. I filled my days swatting ineffectually at swarms of midges that always seemed to go for the tender skin around the eyes and I concentrated on the routine household and garden chores. I took short walks with Samson, whose arthritis was becoming worse – although he still seemed to love a gentle stroll along the roadside with me. He'd snuffle in the grass along the sides of the ditches, gently wagging his tail as he waddled along.

When William did appear, everything and anything seemed to act as an irritant. Minerva drove him mad with her constant swearing.

With distaste, he looked over to where the parrot dozed, hunched on its perch like a tatty, miniature vulture.

"Why you had to rescue that wretched bird, I'll never know. It isn't useful or decorative. It looks ghastly with half its feathers missing and it's foul-mouthed. Why can't you put the cage outside in the daytime for the summer at least?"

"We tried that the first year," I said in a placatory voice, "and she caught a chill and nearly died. Poor thing! Do you remember? I had to give her cognac from an eggcup to revive her."

"She's not even in good enough condition to stick in a casserole."

"William!"

With perfect timing, Minerva sprang into action at the far side of the room screaming, "Bugger, bugger, bugger that bird."

I couldn't help laughing. My husband observed her coldly.

"You see what I mean? Why couldn't it have picked up some decent language from us? Why does the damn bird only remember swear words it picked up from zookeepers?" He rubbed his trousers with an impatient hand. "The bloody dog's as bad. There are Samson's hairs all over the place. I'm sure he got into the bedroom while I was away."

Quickly changing the subject, I commented brightly, "You've failed to notice that you've used 'damn' and 'bloody' in the last thirty seconds. Better be careful or she'll lead us astray. Minerva's influence might be stronger than you think!"

But William was in no mood to be amused.

I never found out what it was that made him more distant than ever. Of course, I didn't know then about his involvement with Veronica but I was sure that something was preying on his mind and stopping him from sleeping.

I think it was around that time that William gave up

going to church. He'd gone nearly every Sunday for as long as I had known him. I was just a Christmas and Easter visitor to the pretty little Protestant church, tucked into a fold of green in the next valley. When I commented on his change of routine, he grew angry.

"If you had made any sort of commitment to a spiritual inner life, Katherine, you would know that one doesn't have to be seen to sit in a church to nourish it. I'm tired of listening to a handful of people singing out of tune and a rector who suffers from halitosis and who can't seem to string a few coherent words together for an intelligent sermon. And what's more, I'm more than bored with the rector's wife playing the part of sweet-natured Lady Bountiful when she's nothing but an empty-headed gossip. I've decided to do my praying at home in future – away from silly distractions."

"Won't you miss it at all? I thought you rather liked some of the regulars," I commented, unconvinced.

"Far from it! There's a happy-clappy element creeping in that's really absurd and now David's died, I don't feel there are any kindred spirits left."

I'd met old David Mayfield a couple of times. He too had been a lecturer at Trinity but nearly thirty years earlier. He was dryly academic with the sort of analytical mind that William admired. The two men occasionally went for a drink together in the local pub after the Sunday service. William, like many other men I'd met, didn't go in for platonic friendships and certainly not for any sort of male bonding. However, the other's death earlier in the year had upset him more than he'd let on.

"Would you like it if I came with you for company?"

He looked at me in surprise. "Why would you do that?"

"I thought I could be a kindred spirit for you. United against the happy-clappy brigade!"

"But you're not a kindred spirit, Katherine. You've never really believed in God or prayer. You only pray when you're upset or want something badly."

This was true. I knew that but why did he have to make me feel so painfully excluded? It occurred to me that I didn't know him any better after over twenty years together than I had at the beginning of our marriage.

"I'd hoped that I *was* a kindred spirit in some ways. It makes me sad when you seem to want to deny any closeness between us. We don't make love any more. We don't even sleep in the same bed, William! And you don't seem to mind."

"Our not sharing the same bedroom has nothing whatsoever to do with my decision over the church issue. Why do you always have to be so emotive?"

Yet again, where I had wanted harmony, I'd only succeeded in alienating William further. I was starting to despair of ever understanding him. I'd never felt more alone. It seemed as though I would have to rely on Samson and Minerva to cheer me up – them, my friends in the book club and the odd visit from Veronica.

Veronica would appear, unannounced, waving a bottle of good red wine and some meaty, black olives or a jar of freshly made houmus from her local delicatessen. She was like a sudden summer storm – upon us before we realised, noisy, invigorating, and then departing as quickly as she had come, leaving us feeling a little bruised by the experience.

She never said or did anything to make me suspect something was going on between them. Sometimes William was there when she arrived, sometimes not, but Veronica always managed to convey the feeling that she was genuinely pleased to see me even when he wasn't there.

"Kate! How lovely! It's been *months* since we had time for a chinwag."

It might have been three weeks but a dash of hyperbole was all part of Veronica's charm. She'd scatter the kitchen table with her purchases and make for the drawer where she'd unearth the corkscrew. Before I had time to say anything much, she'd have poured out two generous helpings of wine, kicked off her high heels and launched into a high-speed monologue of what she'd been doing at work and why Louise from marketing was 'such a wagon'. She would let fall a deluge of famous names with whom she'd been sipping cocktails in the Shelbourne after casting sessions. She would go into a lengthy explanation as to why she was broke because she hadn't been able to resist a *simply wicked* dress by John Rocha. When I think about it, her vocabulary had always been peppered with phrases like that; she still said the sort of things young ones in their teens and twenties might come out with. Monologue over, she'd then lean forward, elbows resting on the table, hands cupping her chin and give me her full attention.

"Enough about me! What have *you* been up to? You hermit, you!"

"Oh, this and that. Nothing to compare with the life you lead," I'd find myself murmuring, rather lamely. The truth was, I couldn't begin to compete with all her goings-on – and didn't particularly want to.

Shortly after things had deteriorated badly between

William and myself, Veronica asked, innocently, if everything was all right.

"You're looking rather worn, if you don't mind me saying, Kate. Is everything OK with you and William?"

It was said in such a concerned way it made it easy for me to talk freely.

"Not really! I've always found it difficult to get close to him. You know how he pushes me away. Lately, it's been worse and I don't know why. We're even sleeping in separate bedrooms now."

"Oh, Kate! I'm so sorry. Do you think I could say anything . . . try and find out what's worrying him?"

She got up and put her arm around my shoulders. I blinked back tears and took a swig of wine.

"No, I expect it'll sort itself out. I'm just being stupid. If he won't discuss things with his own wife, I don't think he'll talk to you."

Ha! Little did I know. She was probably the only person he *did* talk things over with. They must have been over two years into their relationship when I said that! It's beginning to dawn on me that perhaps Veronica's amoral rather than immoral. That would explain her ability to seem to care I was upset and for her to be so warmly generous on the one hand and on the other, to be perfectly at ease while she juggled her affair with William and the other men in her life. Oh, yes! I don't know if he knew it but he wasn't the only man with whom she slept. She told me about some of them.

"Wankers, the lot of them!" she'd laugh, pouring herself another glass of wine. "They all cheat on their wives and yet they think they're God's gift to womankind. Just because a woman's still single at my age, they think they're doing you a tremendous favour by trying to haul you into bed with them. If I ever find myself in danger of falling in love with one of the unmarried ones, I just remind myself of how ridiculous they look just wearing socks and a vest. That keeps me safe from ever ending up washing their damn socks."

"Have you ever been in love, Veronica?" I asked her during one of our sessions.

"Once," she replied, thoughtfully.

"And . . ." I prompted.

"Nothing to report, Kate. It was painful and in the end, bloody. Took me a long time to get over it. I won't ever allow anyone to invade my life in that way again."

"Aren't you afraid of a lonely old age?"

"Nope! I'll do what one of the characters did in a marvellous novel by Colette. She spent thirty odd years as a very beautiful courtesan, much in demand, wined and dined in all the best places. She stored away all the diamonds and gold trinkets they gave her and then, when she decided the time had come, she cut her long hair, dressed in comfortable clothes and flat shoes, tippled Pernod and played cards with her women friends. She was just as content. Seems the perfect recipe for a happy life, if you ask me. Then, if I get to a point when it all becomes too uncomfortable, I'll arrange to be run over by a passing milk float. That *didn't* happen to the Colette character, by the way!"

"Somehow, I can't imagine you in flat shoes and comfortable clothes, swigging Pernod and playing cards. You'll always smell of Chanel No.5 and have smooth, waxed legs. If *you* get run over by anything, I bet it will be a

51

Porsche. You'll never let yourself go – you're not the type," I said.

She gave me a rather enigmatic smile and then said in a low voice,

"Ah, Kate, I don't think anyone knows what other people are really capable of doing or being. Perhaps it's just as well."

From the point of view of our relationship, it was a very good thing I didn't know what she was up to. I wonder what I would have done if I'd known. Would I have taken the easy way out yet again and pretended I didn't? I had shut my eyes and ears so often when Celia needed my support, perhaps I would have been equally as passive about William and Veronica's affair.

Chapter Six

When Celia was five, she started going to the local village school. I managed to persuade William that it would be the best thing for her while she was so young.

"As long as you realise it can only be for a couple of years. She has to go to a proper school in Dublin when she's eight," he warned me.

"The village school *is* a 'proper' school," I said. "It's got terrific facilities, computers, the lot."

"The village school is run by an ex-priest who's a megalomaniac and a neurotic ex-nun and the children all have appalling Wicklow accents – or hadn't you noticed?"

"What does it matter if they do? As long as Celia's happy and gets a good start in all the basics. She does live here and it would be nice for her to have local friends. I don't want her to be cut off from the children in the village."

"The implication being that, once again, I do not know what's best for my own daughter."

"No, William, I didn't mean that at all," I said, wearily.

One of my reasons for wanting Celia to go to school the minute she was five was to get her away from her father. He never seemed to be able to relax and enjoy his daughter. Everything she loved doing, he criticised. As she grew, I could see her becoming less and less sure of herself. William would stand over her, monitoring, insisting on showing her that anything she did could be done much better using his way. I felt that he was stifling her – not giving her room to breathe. It had got to the point where, every time he came into the room, if Celia was there, she would make some excuse or other to go to her bedroom or into the garden, anywhere, as long as it was away from his watchful eye.

"I want to have Sam on my bed tonight, Mummy," she pleaded, the day before she was due to start at her new school.

I knew that much as she was looking forward to the experience, she was a little nervous.

"I think you could as a special treat."

"Absolutely out of the question," said William.

"Daddy! Please?"

"No, Celia. It's unhygienic."

"What's that mean?"

"It means Sam's not clean."

Celia looked up at her father with big smile.

"He *is*, Daddy! Mummy gave him a bath and he smells lovely and clean."

William turned to me abruptly.

"The dog does not sleep on her bed."

Exit William. End of discussion. Tears of rage from Celia, who refused to let me comfort her.

"Why can't I have him? I like cuddling Sam. Why can't I?"

"Daddy's right, darling. He does leave dog-hairs all over the place."

"I don't care! I love Sam. Daddy doesn't let me do *anything* I want!"

"Celia, don't say that. Daddy wants what's good for you."

"Sam's good for me," she replied, mutinously.

I tried to persuade her to come to me for a hug but she pushed my hands away.

"You don't help me. *You* could let me have Sam on my bed."

But I couldn't or felt I couldn't. I'd become frightened of my own husband.

In fact, the village school episode only lasted six months. One day, during the Easter term, Celia came home in tears. She flung herself at me, sobbing.

"Whatever's the matter, darling?"

"Miss Farringdon said I was going to Hell."

"She said *what?*"

"She said that Jesus died on the cross so that all the Catholics could go to Heaven and because I wasn't a Catholic there wasn't any room for me in Heaven. She said that people who weren't Catholics burn in Hell," she repeated, miserably. "I don't want to go to Hell."

"Of course you're not going to Hell. You must have made a mistake."

At that moment, William came into the room.

"What's the matter?" he asked, full of concern.

"There's been some sort of a misunderstanding at school. Don't worry, I'll sort it out."

"What sort of a misunderstanding?"

There was a silence.

"Well?"

With a sense of foreboding, I replied, "Celia's got the wrong end of the stick and thinks that she's not going to be allowed into Heaven. It's just a silly mix-up. I'll speak to Miss Farringdon tomorrow morning."

William ignored me, putting a hand on his daughter's shoulder.

"Celia? Tell me exactly what happened."

Holding tightly onto my hand, she told him. When she'd finished, he turned to me, grim-faced.

"Right! I'm not waiting until tomorrow. I'm going down to speak to that woman right now. No one tells a five-year-old child she will go to Hell because she doesn't happen to have been baptised into the Catholic faith. No one!"

I don't know what was said that afternoon but Celia never went back.

Three weeks later, she was enrolled into a smart Dublin school of William's choice.

"Much more satisfactory. She won't have to face any bigotry there," he said, looking pleased with himself.

And William was right. Old Hall was a multi-denominational establishment run by a liberal-minded headmistress who believed, rather like Miss Jean Brodie, that *all* her girls would be successful. You found out what a pupil was good at, pointed them in the right direction, nurtured them, encouraged them and then sent them out into the world at eighteen, full of confidence and ready for anything.

I liked Miss Henry, the headmistress, very much. She

was a tall beanpole of a woman with grey hair combed back into a tidy twist on top of her head. She had a penchant for brightly coloured, hand-knitted cardigans, was a shrewd judge of character and intensely interested in all the girls in her care. Although she taught in the senior school, Miss H, as she was referred to by nearly everyone, knew all forty individual children in the junior school by name.

After a week, I could see that Celia loved being there, even though the long car journey each morning and evening meant she was exhausted by the time we got home. She hardly saw her father during term time and I sadly realised that it seemed better that way – she appeared to be so much happier than before. Celia seemed to fill out, become more robust and bonny looking. She would talk practically non-stop all the way home each day, telling me all the things she'd been doing and describing who had said what to whom. It was lovely to see her so animated.

One afternoon, about ten days after her starting at Old Hall, Celia came running to the car as soon as I arrived to collect her. She looked out of breath and excited. I could see that she was pulling a diminutive, dark-haired child along by the hand.

"Mummy, this is Becky! She's my best friend. Can she come to tea?"

I laughed. "Hello, Becky. I'm afraid there wouldn't be time for you to come to tea today because it takes ages to drive to our house. Perhaps you'd like to come and see Celia at the weekend?"

Dark eyes regarded me thoughtfully from under a thick fringe of hair, making me think of a small mouse, peering out from under the eaves of a thatched cottage.

She nodded solemnly then released herself from Celia's grip, mumbling, "'Bye," and ran over to a shiny blue Range Rover that had just swung in the gate, scattering gravel onto the rose beds. I glimpsed an elegant woman with red hair at the wheel. Her face seemed faintly familiar. The car door had barely shut when the vehicle drove off again.

That night, when Celia had gone to bed, I asked William whether he minded if the new best friend came out at the weekend. His response was not particularly enthusiastic.

"You know I need peace and quiet when I'm writing and two children racing around the place will make it impossible for me to work."

"Well," I said, "I thought that if the weather was OK, I'd take them down to the fun park at Claragh. Celia loves going there. I'll do my best to keep them out of your way."

Even while I spoke those conciliatory words I was thinking, 'Young children make noise – that's what they do – it's normal! Your book can wait. Why can't you put your daughter first for once? *Why* do the pair of us have to behave like insignificant little satellites, orbiting around your sun all the time?'

Reluctantly, he agreed that I could speak to Becky's mother and see what she thought. I got the feeling he was hoping the woman would say 'Thank you, but no.'

The next day, I spoke to Becky's red-haired mother who said there would be no problem, asked for directions and promised to drop the child out by eleven on Saturday morning. I still had the feeling I'd seen her before but she showed no sign of recognising me so I didn't say anything.

Celia was ecstatic and spent the Friday evening brushing Sam so that he would 'look smart for Becky'. I managed to persuade her that half strangling him with a blue ribbon was not a good idea; that he looked more handsome wearing just his own, old leather collar. She was so happy, she forgot to argue.

She was up and dressed by six that Saturday morning. I was woken by Sam, barking in the garden. Hastily putting on my dressinggown, I crept out of the bedroom and made my way down the passage towards the kitchen. Celia was perched on a stool, pouring cereal into a bowl. She greeted me with a broad smile.

"Hello, Mummy. I did all my buttons up!"

"Celia! It's only six in the morning. The birds aren't even awake yet."

"I let Sam out for his pee too."

"I know. He woke me up and if we don't get him inside quickly, he'll wake Daddy up as well."

When Sam had been let in, I thought I might as well join my daughter for breakfast and hope that William had not been disturbed. We sat side by side at the table while Celia chattered happily about all the things she wanted to show Becky when she came and what they wanted to do at the fun park. Her excitement was contagious.

As it turned out, the day was a disaster. Celia became frantic when Becky hadn't arrived by a quarter-past eleven.

"Mummy, why isn't she here?" she wailed, driving her exasperated father into his study, clutching a cup of black coffee.

"Just be patient. You know how sometimes the traffic is bad in Dublin or there are sheep all over the road at this end. She'll be here soon. Don't worry!"

When nothing had happened by a quarter-to-twelve, Celia burst into tears.

"Becky's not coming!"

Just then, to my relief, the blue Range Rover appeared in the drive. William had erupted into the kitchen to remonstrate over the fuss Celia was making. He looked through the window, in time to see Becky's mother climbing out of the car. Then he was gone. Back to his study without a word. His behaviour didn't strike me as strange until I thought about it later. I was too busy trying to open the door with one hand while holding back a barking Sam, who had suddenly become all territorial, with the other.

The two girls immediately disappeared in the direction of Celia's bedroom. Becky's mother gave me a brief smile and said she couldn't stop. She had an appointment in town. I was asked when would I like her to collect her daughter. I said I would drop Becky in myself so that she didn't have to do two runs but she dismissed the suggestion and said I was very kind but she'd prefer to collect her herself. I found myself wondering if someone had told her that I was a dangerous driver and not to be trusted in a car with small children.

Then the rain started. Not just your average shower but a heavy, continuous downpour that hid the mountains and made the lawn into a bog within half an hour. They were very good at first: playing with dolls, drawing, grooming a reluctant Sam who tried hiding, unsuccessfully, under the kitchen table. Then they asked for some old clothes so they could dress up.

Foolishly, I let them into our bedroom. I thought that as it was the room furthest away from William's study, it was the best place for them to be and it wouldn't matter if they got a bit rowdy.

Sometime later, I went to check that all was well. When I opened the bedroom door, I was knocked back by a powerful smell. I knew immediately what it was. It was the expensive perfume Veronica had given me for my birthday and that I kept for special occasions. An empty perfume bottle lay on the ground at the feet of two very guilty-looking children. Becky was dressed in my old summer dressing-gown with a large sun hat and dark glasses, looking rather like a small Madam Arcarty. Celia had decided against wearing any of the garments I'd put out on the bed for them. Instead, she'd managed to open the wardrobe door and pull down one of the only two smart suits William owned. The jacket arms hung down to the carpet and the trousers collapsed in folds around her ankles with the waistband held in place under her armpits by a tightly knotted silk tie. The whole ensemble reeked of *Joy*.

Of course it was at that precise moment that William appeared in the doorway. He always seemed to have an uncanny knack of materialising when things had gone disastrously wrong and before I'd had time to take any sort of remedial action. He sniffed the air and then surveyed the scene in front of him, his eyes finally coming to rest on Celia's outfit. He let out a roar which made all three of us jump.

"What the *hell* is going on in here?"

He looked at me as though I had orchestrated the whole thing.

From then on, it was downhill all the way. I'd grilled fish

fingers with baked beans for lunch because that was one of Celia's favourite meals. The two girls were so traumatised by the verbal lashing they'd received, neither of them would eat more than a few mouthfuls. William, breathing heavily, prodded a fish finger with his fork, looking as though he expected it to leap off the plate and poke him in the eye. I rather wished it would.

Sam had eaten something unspeakable he'd found in the garden and was sick all over the rush matting by the fire in the middle of lunch. Then, because the children hadn't eaten their first course, William informed them that they couldn't have any pudding. So my carefully concocted chocolate fudge cake with cream, that I'd slaved over late into the previous night, stayed where it was in the fridge.

In the afternoon, in a state of advanced desperation, I packed children and dog into the car and drove around the mountains in the rain, brightly pointing out interesting landmarks. Mind you, the landmarks were nearly all completely obscured by rain and the girls were stubbornly silent, determined not to be in the slightest bit interested.

Exhausted, I eventually drove home through lakes of water and gushing torrents that spouted out of unexpected places in the hedgerows. The poor car bumped in and out of submerged potholes so that I started to wonder if we'd make it back in one piece.

After a silent tea, I parked them in front of the telly, turned down low so that there would be no more fireworks from William. Eventually, Becky's mother reappeared. As before, she wouldn't stay, but stood by the door. It was almost as if she was waiting for William to appear. She obviously wasn't interested in talking to me. She kept glancing in the direction of his study with an expectant look on her face. It was only afterwards that it occurred to me that it was strange she should know from which direction my husband would appear, if he decided to. However, William stayed firmly put. I couldn't help noticing how beautiful she was, even in a mac and headscarf.

As I waved them off down the path, I heard Becky say in a loud voice, "I don't like them."

As we came back into the house, Celia burst into tears and Sam was sick again, only this time over my boots lying by the back door.

Later, in bed that night, I finally remembered where I'd last seen Becky's beautiful mother. It was three or four years earlier when I'd dropped in to William's rooms in Trinity. Something had arrived in the post that I knew he'd been waiting for. I thought he'd like to get his hands on it sooner rather than later. He hadn't been expecting me and when I opened the door of his college room, they were standing very close to each other. I knew from the expression on their faces that they hadn't been discussing tutorials.

"Claire's just leaving," was all he said, as he ushered her past me.

When she'd gone, he said, "I'm extremely busy, Katherine. You know I don't like it when you arrive unexpectedly like this."

I gave him the packet and believe it or not, *I* was the one who apologised. Flushed and miserable, I then left, feeling foolish and in the way.

Was William still seeing her? I wondered miserably. I didn't understand how someone who spent so much of his time praying, could also be unfaithful – but I never summoned up enough courage to confront him. Why?

Chapter Seven

I've discovered that The Presence is my Guardian Angel, that he's a he and that he's black! And he's lovely! I haven't *seen* him in the conventional sense but his voice has become so clear in my mind. It has a rich, deep, chocolate sort of resonance to it. His name is Thomas Adeola and we've just had the most amazing discussion.

As soon as he knew I was desperate to understand why William had been the way he was, that I *really* wanted to know, he said he would do his best to show me.

I wasn't prepared for the method he used. All of a sudden, it was as though I had a miniature television screen inside my head. Instead of hovering over the world like I had been getting used to, I was able to hear and see and be close to what was happening in this new, other place.

The first image appears: a young boy – he looks about nine or ten – is being locked into a scantily furnished room by a fat, middle-aged man with a bald head. The man wears small, round glasses that are almost sliding off his red nose. It looks to me as though its owner is no stranger to the bottle. The rest of his face is an unbecoming purple, marbled by little blue veins. He's shouting angrily through the door.

"You'll stay there until you've written it out one hundred times, 'The family that prays together stays together,' and just you remember that if your godforsaken parents had done that, you wouldn't be here now, making my life a misery."

The boy in the room is silent. He has a long, pale face with dark brown, unhappy eyes and his hair is black. I immediately recognise William's slim-wristed hands with the two-inch scar down one side of the left hand where he told me he'd cut himself with a knife when he was seven.

He walks slowly to the other side of the room and sits down at the small table near the window, picks up a pen and starts to write. His face is expressionless as if he's withdrawn inside himself so that no one can find out what he's thinking.

The scene in front of me is so real, I feel I could reach out and touch him. I wish I could communicate with this other William. He looks so . . . vulnerable.

Then the picture fades and is replaced by another room. A single overhead light shines on the back and shoulders of the fat man I saw earlier. He's dressed in old-fashioned, striped pyjamas and is kneeling beside a bed, his head in his hands. I hear him muttering; a low, monotonous stream of words and I realise that he's praying. I don't know how long the man stays kneeling on the bare boards beside the iron frame bed, but he seems to be there for ages. The words 'sin' and 'sinful' crop up rather a lot. I wonder, is he referring to William or to himself?

And now, another scene: early morning, I think, because the low sun is shining on roofs still white with frost. William and the man are hurrying towards a tall, grey church.

"You haven't eaten, I hope?" The man still sounds angry.

"No, Uncle Joseph."

"Did you drink anything?"

"No, Uncle Joseph," says William again in an expressionless voice that matches his face.

So, the fat man is William's uncle. He's never mentioned the name Joseph to me, or the fact that he even had an uncle. Judging from the evidence so far, I'm not surprised. The man looks full of hate. I can feel it rising from him in great, vaporous waves, like steam from a grating over some hellish, subterranean kitchen.

"Well, I don't believe you. You're always telling lies. I expect you sneaked into the kitchen when I wasn't around, didn't you? You think you're so clever but you'll learn."

The man sounds extraordinarily menacing. As they climb the steps up to the church doors, he suddenly stops and rounds on William, who flinches.

"No Holy Communion for you until you've made a proper and full confession. Do you understand?"

"Yes."

"Yes, what?"

"Yes, Uncle Joseph."

The picture changes yet again: this time, the screen shows a young woman, crying quietly. She sits on the end of a bed in what looks like a hotel room. Not a very nice one. She has long, dark hair that falls untidily over her bare shoulders and from what I can see of her, even though she's distressed, she looks attractive. There are a handful of bank notes lying on the bed beside her. She's only half-dressed and I can see bruises on her arms. I don't have to be shown anything else. I know that she's just been paid for services rendered.

She lifts her head and I'm shocked to see she has the same-shaped face, the same dark eyes and the identical withdrawn look that I've just witnessed on the face of the young boy in the last scene. I know that she is William's mother.

Before I have time to think, she fades and William appears again. He too is crying but now his face is contorted with pain and his eyes are wide open and unfocussed. The boy's knuckles are white from holding onto the end of an iron-frame bed. Trousers and underpants are around his ankles and the fat man is behind him, holding him down on the bed by his bony shoulders.

I want to wipe away this horror in my head but the picture stays brutally vivid.

Finally, the man called Joseph climbs off William and buttons his trousers. He hauls the sobbing boy up by one arm and gives him a shake.

"That's the right treatment for the son of a drunkard and a whore. Go to your room. You disgust me."

Hanging on the wall above the bed, I see a wooden crucifix.

Suddenly, the screen has disappeared and I am enveloped in

Thomas's comforting presence. I feel weak and shaken by what he has just shown me.

"I didn't know!" I cry out. "He never said *anything* to me about all of that."

I want to weep but Thomas's voice tells me to be still, be calm.

"Do you begin to understand?"

"Yes!" I say, "Yes! It explains a lot of things but why did this make him want to be with other women? Was I such a bad wife to him?"

"You too were unfaithful."

"I know but my infidelity was joyful and only with one man – and only for such a short time."

"Does that make any difference? Infidelity is infidelity. Where I came from, people were killed if they committed adultery."

"Do you think that was right?" I ask, roused.

"It was the custom of that place at that time."

"So, what you're saying is that one should play by the rules, even if the rules are wrong?"

"There have to be rules, otherwise anarchy prevails and the weak suffer even more."

"I did love him at the beginning, you know."

"I know that and I think you never really stopped loving him. That is why he was able to hurt you so much. He tried to love you, Kate."

"No! He may have at first but William hasn't tried to love me for a long, long time. He wouldn't have had a ten-year affair with my best friend if he'd cared the smallest bit for me."

"And how do you feel about her now?"

"I think you know very well how I feel about Veronica!"

"Do you intend to push her into any more holes in the ground?"

I may be wrong but I think there was just the faintest hint of a smile in his voice when he asked me that.

"I hadn't really given it much thought." I pause. "I got the impression that things got a little chilly up here the last time I did that."

There was a velvet chuckle.

"I'm not the only one around up here, you know. We angels are all different, with different approaches to our different problems."

"So, you see me as your problem, do you?"

"I think you see yourself as a problem. You are dissatisfied and unsure of what you were and are still. Look at it like this: you are on a learning curve and if you really wish to understand, you will learn. As the man said, 'All will be well.'.

"Well, yes, I suppose I do see myself as a problem and I'm sorry you should have been lumbered with me. I suppose it's a case of everyone having their own cross to bear. Oh! Sorry. I didn't mean . . ."

"That's quite all right," says Thomas in his calm, chocolate voice. "No offence taken."

He's left me to myself for a bit. I think he wants me to work it out on my own about just what I have to do next. I really meant what I said to him. I do want to understand William. I feel appalled that he should have had to live, is still living, through life with all that ghastly baggage from his childhood.

William told me, shortly before we married, that his parents were both dead. I'm sure they are now but I wonder if they were back then? He must have been terrified of me finding out about his mother. No wonder the name of Joseph was never mentioned.

What I find difficult to understand is why didn't he seek professional help? He needn't have told me. It would have been easy for him to see someone in Dublin when he worked there for so much of the time. I suppose his pride stopped him from talking about something that was, to him, so overwhelmingly shameful.

Is it possible that William had affairs because, at the back of his mind, he hoped that he would find a woman who was chaste, who'd turn him down? A woman who was the opposite of his mother. Or was it that he thought her behaviour was typical of all women; that all women are whores at heart? How ironic that I proved him right when it came to my test of faithfulness.

When I saw him that night after the funeral, the thing that struck me hardest was his loneliness. It's ridiculous! It doesn't have to be that way. He has a daughter somewhere out in that world down there and there's a good chance *she* may be alone too. I think what I've got to do now is find Celia. Then I have to somehow get the two of them together. Perhaps that'll prove impossible and if I do succeed, maybe their meeting will be a complete disaster – but I have to try. Will Thomas help me?

Chapter Eight

I ask Thomas, "How come I have a Guardian Angel when I hardly ever went to church and found it next to impossible to believe in God?"

He sounds amused.

"Do you think He is petty enough to worry about labels? You tried to do your best . . . most of the time . . . and that's what counts up here."

"Well, that's a relief! I thought that if Heaven *did* exist and you wanted to get in, you had to belong to some sort of organised religion to be eligible."

"Girl!" His amusement is even more evident. "You make it sound as though you think people down there are all queuing up to get into some sort of fancy Country Club. It's not like that at all!"

"You'd be surprised by what people down there think!"

"No, I don't think so. Nothing surprises us up here. We become very sad sometimes at the foolishness of the world but not surprised."

"What about people, like Celia's teacher, who told her she would go to Hell because she wasn't a Catholic?"

There was a pause and then he says, "Yes, we were aware of Miss Farringdon's narrow views on such matters. Brother Raphael has his work cut out for him there but he's slowly making progress. The Almighty loves a good Catholic but He is not a Catholic, Kate. He finds some of their dogmas a little hard to swallow."

"So, there's hope for everybody then?"

"Of course there is!"

"Won't an awful lot of people feel let down when they've worked hard to lead good lives, play by the rules, whatever, when they find out that their God is not what they thought?"

"Let us just say that they get over their shock very quickly when they discover the truth. Joyful, not shocked, is how I would describe their state on finding out what is what."

"And Hell?" I ask, somewhat tentatively.

"What about it?"

"I'd just like to know that Breughel and Bosch got it wrong."

That marvellous chuckle again. "They got it wrong but they frightened a lot of people into living quite passable lives and it was back in the sixteenth century, don't forget!"

"But, doesn't there always have to be a balance in things? Good versus Evil. If there's a Heaven, then there must be a Hell, surely?"

"Kate, when you were a young child with loving parents who provided you with all your needs: love, warmth, guidance, nourishment – all the things you required to develop and become strong. Can you imagine the terror of that same child if she were to be lost, unloved, cold, blind, deaf and adrift in a state of infinite isolation?

"Yes," I reply, with a shiver.

"Then you have a very rough idea of what it would be like to be in what you call Hell."

"And is there no hope for the people who are in that state?"

"There is always hope. Redemption is possible – even there." There is a silence and then Thomas asks, "What is it you want me to help you do?"

"Will you help me bring William and Celia together?"

"I will give you as much guidance as I am allowed to give but it is you, Kate, who must search for Celia; do the spade work as it were. You are already aware of your increased mental agility and how you can transport yourself to where you want to be."

"I find my new-found mobility a little shocking sometimes. I'm not always prepared for where I end up or the speed at which I get there," I comment, thinking of my precipitous arrival in Veronica's bedroom a few days earlier.

"You will get better at it. Don't worry! As the song says . . ."

"I know! 'Don't worry, be happy!'"

"Nice bit of rhythm in that song, I always thought," said Thomas. "If only the people down there spent more of their time singing and dancing, they wouldn't have so much energy left with which to be foolish."

Then I'm aware of him withdrawing – not leaving me completely – more as though he were standing back, waiting to see what I will do next.

I suppose I was hoping for some more of those mind

pictures, so that it would make it easier for me to find Celia. (Even though I hadn't liked what Thomas showed me.) Then I remember how I'd thought of Veronica and instantly been in the room with her. I have been trying hard *not* to think of her – kinder on both her and me – and Zaza – that way. So I start to concentrate on Celia.

The trouble is, I haven't seen her for eight years and all I can recall is how she looked in a handful of photos taken the year before she went away. Her face is no longer familiar to me – or her voice. I do remember her mannerisms though: the way she'd brush her hair back impatiently with her hand like William still does, how she'd sit on the window seat with her arms wrapped around Sam, gazing out towards the mountains. The way she always frowned with concentration when she had to play a particularly difficult passage on the flute. Celia had a way of leaning towards the music stand and giving a little movement with her head at the start of a phrase. Her face took on a remote quality when she played. She'd never hear the phone ringing or the front door bell.

I don't suppose that now she's at all how I remember her to have looked. I concentrate on thinking of my fair-haired daughter with the freckles she so hated, scattered over the bridge of her nose like sesame seeds on a freshly baked bread roll. I think of her unusual blue eyes that always made me think of the colour of the sea in one of the little beaches in Corfu where William and I spent our honeymoon. Celia's eyes and silky, long blonde hair were her best assets physically. She resented the fact that she'd inherited my shortness of stature.

"Why am I so small?" she'd groan, standing on tiptoe. When she was about twelve, I several times found her doing stretching exercises in front of her bedroom mirror. She even tried hanging from the branch of a tree, wearing her heaviest walking shoes and with stones in her pockets to weigh her down, when she thought no one was looking.

I thought of how Celia had sat on my lap while I read to her every night until, at the age of six, she could read most of the words in her favourite books herself. Almost overnight, I became redundant.

"Me can read myself," she said, pulling the book away from me.

I'd watch her as she followed the lines of text with her finger, her mouth shaping the most difficult words. She quickly grew more and more adept. William was as impressed as I was although he didn't say much. I saw him hesitating between the work waiting for him in his study and pretending to be busy in the kitchen, all the time with an eye on his clever daughter. And she was clever. That's what made him so angry later on when she wouldn't work during her last year at school.

There were just too many things to do and too many people to distract her from her schoolwork. As she got older, Celia seemed to act as confidante to several of her friends, male and female. By the time she was sixteen, she'd learned how to escape from her father and me by joining any clubs she could. She belonged to the school camera club, the drama group, the debating society and the choir. It was at school that she developed a crush on the music teacher. There was a vacancy for a flautist in the school orchestra – so Celia started to learn the flute. She threw herself into her music studies in a way that left little time for other work and it gave William yet another reason to criticise and be angry.

"She'll fail her Leaving," he said, the month before Celia sat her exams. "She'll fail and then she won't have enough points to get into Trinity."

"She doesn't want to go to Trinity, William," I said, for the umpteenth time.

"What Celia wants and what is good for her are two very different things."

A school report at the end of the previous term had just about summed up the situation as far as William was concerned. It said: 'Celia seems to think that school is one long coffee break.' I'd thought that a rather witty observation but her father was not amused. Neither was Miss Henry.

"Celia has so much going for her. Everyone likes her, staff and the other girls, and she's as bright as a button. What is making her switch off from her studies?"

She had asked me to go in and see her. Really, she'd wanted to see both William and me but he was away at the time. This gave me the freedom to try and explain, in a way that would have been impossible if he'd been there too.

"I'm afraid that Celia is feeling very antagonised by her parents at the moment."

Miss Henry leaned towards me, pulling her bright red and blue cardigan more closely around her shoulders.

"A lot of teenage girls go through the stage of thinking their parents know nothing. They can be very intolerant and unforgiving of perceived parental flaws. However, I would have expected Celia to have knuckled down during her final year. She knows how important it is to have good exam results. After all, you and your husband have given her the best possible start in life by sending her to Old Hall."

"I know," I said, "but the trouble is that her father's a little . . ."

"Autocratic?" Miss Henry suggested, gently. "Yes, I had noticed a slight tendency on Mr Fitzgerald's part to expect Celia to toe the line, however strongly she felt about a topic."

The discussion ended with Miss Henry suggesting Celia should be allowed to say what she thought about it all. She said William should be encouraged to listen and then to possibly agree to come to a compromise and that Celia should be allowed to make some decisions on where her life was leading. Then she would perhaps be more amenable to any suggestions her father might make. It sounded a good idea at the time.

I reported carefully selected extracts from our conversation over the phone to William later that night. I made the point that Celia might not know what she wanted but she was very clear on the subject of what she didn't want.

"The trouble with you, Katherine, is that you're as immature as she is. You've never grown up and so are in no position to judge the situation competently."

So nothing had changed. William was as unbending as ever but Celia showed that she too could stick to her guns. The result was an impasse with me, twittering on the sidelines, frightened to upset either one of them by suggesting anything at all. Oh, it was dreadful!

I realise that I've spent so much time remembering, I've got sidetracked and forgotten to concentrate on finding Celia. I close my invisible eyes and try again.

Slowly, I feel a change in the light – as though someone

has pulled back curtains and allowed the sunshine in. The air around me has become warm and I can smell the scent of flowers.

I look down and see that I am drifting over a white-walled house with blue shutters and a rose-coloured pantiled roof. The house is surrounded by a wild garden with roughly cut grass, a clothesline with washing pegged out on it and scrub and bracken invading the outer edge of the grass. There are some toys lying on the ground near the house and a brightly coloured ball has rolled up against one of the walls. A couple of pine trees stand in a corner of the garden and a large mimosa grows up against the house, close to a window. There's a small terrace with a garden table and two chairs. Growing over the terrace, smothering a sagging pergola, is the most beautiful, purple bougainvillea. Its colour is very rich and ecclesiastical-looking. I'm sure Thomas would like it. The bracken reminds me of Glendalough. It surprises me a little because the temperature tells me I am somewhere a lot further south than Ireland. Could it be France? That's where Celia phoned from when she last made contact with us. To get a better, overall view, I rise up higher into the air, feeling rather like a barrage balloon filled with helium. My manoeuvrings are incredibly silent as well as invisible and I'm getting to be quite a dab hand at controlling my speed and angle of trajectory. In fact, I think that my method of transport is pretty spectacular – no buzzing engine or grinding of gears at all!

I can see that this place is an island. At one end, there's a tall lighthouse. I can also see a port, filled with what look like brightly coloured fishing trawlers. There are striped awnings protecting trestle tables from a hot sun, in an open market on the quayside. People move unhurriedly in and out of the shade, chatting, examining the fruit and vegetables and fish.

There seem to be very few cars moving along the winding, dusty, little roads that criss-cross the island. The roads seem to follow the contours of the land, like ancient sheep trails, rather than attempting to get from A to B using the most direct route. At the meeting of the road coming from the port and the road from the lighthouse is a cluster of houses beside a church. All the houses are built with the same whitewashed walls, blue shutters and pantiled roofs.

All at once, I notice a young woman walking slowly down a track leading to the first house I saw when I got here. She has short blonde hair and is wearing a pretty blue dress that is the colour of the Aegean. I glide closer. Her eyes match her dress.

Chapter Nine

One minute, I'm on an island in full sunshine, studying my daughter's face for clues as to whether she's healthy, happy – anything that will tell me if she's all right or not. Next thing I know, I suddenly find myself back in the clouds with Thomas.

"What did you do *that* for?" I ask, breathlessly.

"Because, dear Kate, I thought you might do something a little precipitous – you were getting so excited."

"Of course I was excited! I'd just seen my daughter for the first time in over eight years. Wouldn't you have been excited if you were me?"

"Yes, I would but there are other matters you must understand before you go back to Celia. There are a few things that should be made clear to you; things that will help you achieve your wish to bring your husband and daughter together. Don't be in too much of a rush. You have all the time in the world."

"That makes you sound rather like Louis Armstrong!"

"Ah, Brother Louis!" Thomas's voice was full of affection.

NICOLA LINDSAY

"There is a queue as long as Africa to get in to *his* cornet and trumpet lessons."

For a moment, I get sidetracked by this amazing image.

"You mean you have music lessons where you are?"

"Of course! Girl, you don't stop learning just because you've died!"

"I always wanted to play the violin," I say, wistfully.

"Mm. So you'd be concentrating on the classical repertoire. I'm more of a jazz person myself. Brother Yehudi is the man for you."

"Brother Yehudi?"

"Oh, yes! You'd probably have known him as Yehudi Menuhin down there. I went to hear him in the early '50's. Great musician! He's applied to go back down as a jazz pianist though."

"So death isn't the end?" My mind starts spinning. "He wants to be reincarnated as a jazz pianist?"

"That's right! We'll sorely miss him up here."

"Will I be reincarnated?" I ask, not so sure that I find the idea all that appealing. "I suppose it wouldn't be too bad if you could choose who you wanted to be."

I have a sudden vision of myself going back as a long-limbed, six-foot-high beauty with an amazingly high IQ and an ability to hold my own in an argument.

"That depends, Kate. You have to have reached a high level of development for you to be considered for that and," he said, reading my unsent thoughts, "if you think about it, being six foot high can lead to back problems and sore heads from low doorways. Anyway, I think you are looking a little too far ahead. Aren't there other matters you should be concentrating on at this moment?"

82

"Well, *I* wanted to stay with Celia and see how things are with her but you brought me back here. Why?"

"Because there is more that you should understand about William. You saw how unhappy his childhood was and now you should know something about his adult life that he hid from you. Something that caused him a lot of anguish."

"You mean the fact that he had women friends? I knew about some of them."

"No," said Thomas. "Not that. I mean William's loss of faith."

"His *what*? I thought his faith was the most important thing in his life. He spent most of his time writing books about religion and spiritual leaders, saints – all that sort of stuff."

"Yes, well. Do you remember how he stopped going to church?"

"I do. He told me he was fed up with all the silly distractions there. I remember he said that you didn't have to be in a church to pray. So I presumed he prayed at home instead. Didn't he?"

"He tried to. He tried very hard but his mind was too full of bitter thoughts and disappointment. That time when you were with Milo, William had gone away on a lecture tour and when he came home, you remember, you thought he was different?"

"Yes. Did something happen while he was away?"

"Nothing happened in the physical sense but all his doubts, his trying to be reconciled with his childhood experiences and the belief that the church, his church, had let him down, all this came to a head. I suppose he had what you would call a sort of breakdown, a spiritual crisis."

I feel stunned. William, of all people!

"I always wondered how he could have relationships outside marriage while still appearing to be so very . . . pious . . . and self-righteous."

Thomas ignores the dig at my husband.

"I want to show you something, Kate. Be still and concentrate."

The screen has come back in my head and I find myself looking at the kitchen at home. Veronica is there. Her tan and sun-bleached hair make her look even more attractive than ever. She's everything I never was. No wonder William likes being with her. Veronica looks as though she's just arrived and is removing a very smart blue coat – which I happen to know is new and cost her a packet. She'd described it to me after seeing it in a fashion show just before I went into hospital.

"I'm going to be strong-minded and not give in. I've got too many coats as it is," she'd said with a laugh.

Seems as though she's not so strong-minded after all!

I can't say I'm too thrilled at seeing my friend again. Especially when she's looking so fantastic and so very – alive and in *my* kitchen with *my* husband.

I hear Thomas's voice.

"Concentrate, Kate. Concentrate!"

I do as I'm told and concentrate. William is sitting at the kitchen table. His expression surprises me. It's one I remember all too clearly – aloof and unfriendly – but I'd never seen him look at Veronica like that before. He used to demonstrate a sort of tolerant amusement whenever she was around. She's walking towards the table and he's not getting up to greet her. That's odd for a start. William always had such good manners in his dealings with other people outside the family.

"William!" she says, in a bright voice but with a slightly reproachful edge to it. "I was expecting you to ring. I told you I was coming back on the seven o'clock flight yesterday. When I tried to phone here, I couldn't get through."

"I knew when you were coming back," says William, in a tone that always used to make me think of Siberian corrective labour camps. "I took the phone off the hook. I've been busy, correcting proofs."

I think of Thomas and try to let all thoughts of, 'Now you know what it feels like, mate!' drain away.

Veronica is looking taken aback.

"But, why take the phone off when we haven't seen each other for three weeks and you knew I'd want to get in touch?"

"Because, frankly I didn't want to hear all about the *marvellous* time you'd had in Portugal and all the *simply amazing* people you'd met there," he snaps.

I know we sometimes used to make fun of the exaggerated way Veronica talked but I think that was a bit cruel.

"Aren't you pleased to see me?" she asks.

"I don't really know why you're here. You weren't invited."

That was most definitely below the belt. What's wrong with him? Veronica sits down on a chair, looking baffled and hurt.

"I came because I've been away for three weeks and I wanted to see you. I needed to be with you. What's wrong, William? What's changed?"

My husband leans back in his chair and gives her a cool, questioning stare.

"Don't you feel just the slightest bit guilty?"

"What should I be feeling guilty about?" she asks, a little nervously, and I *know* she's remembering a man called Alejandro, with whom she's spent a large part of the previous three weeks. He *was* rather gorgeous, judging by the outrageous images that have just popped into her mind.

I honestly think that, for a moment, Veronica really can't imagine, other than Alejandro, why else she should experience any feelings of guilt.

William continues to observe her with a basilisk stare. "The name Katherine springs to mind."

"Oh, Kate!" There's a pause. "What do you want me to say about her?"

"You were supposed to be her best friend, weren't you?"

Immediately, Veronica rallies and retaliates. "*You* were supposed to be her husband but that didn't stop you sleeping with me. I was very fond of Kate but she obviously wasn't the person you wanted to be with in bed when it came to making a choice. The last thing I ever wanted was to upset her but what she didn't know didn't hurt her and it kept you happy. So why are you trying to make me out as the bad guy in all of this? Why should I feel guilty? I've done nothing terrible."

"Why should you feel guilty?" William suddenly drops his gaze and stares unseeingly down at the table. When he speaks, his voice is gentler. "Perhaps I want you to feel the way I do. I'm feeling extraordinarily guilty, Veronica. Guilty about our relationship – and the way I left it to her to try and make our marriage work. She deserved a better husband than me."

"You're feeling guilty because she's just died. I suppose that's only to be expected. You'll get over it."

Good old pragmatic Veronica! I must admit, I used to admire the way she was so very unsentimental about things. It's obviously proving useful in the aftermath of my death but I can see that William finds her attitude unsympathetic.

"But the thing is, Veronica, I don't want to get over it. I don't want to forget her and pretend it didn't matter that I made her miserable." He looks over to an empty dog basket in the corner of the room. "Even old Samson showed her more affection than I did. The day she died, he stopped eating. I found him stretched out, stiff and cold in front of her bedroom door a week later."

Poor, dear Samson! I've been so occupied with the two humans, I hadn't noticed he wasn't around. Veronica is beginning to sound a little impatient. I think I prefer that to her looking all hurt.

"I never thought you'd be the sort of person to wallow in self pity. Would wearing a hair shirt and indulging in a little self-flagellation change what happened? Why spoil what we have by being like this? Kate is *dead* and nothing will bring her back. You can't make it up to her now, William. It's too late for that!" She gets up and goes over to where he's sitting. "Come on! I'm not going to put my life on hold just because she's gone. You're free now to do what you like, without Kate around your neck like an albatross."

I was an albatross, was I? And I'd begun to feel sorry for her.

Impatiently, seeing that agreement between the two of them is obviously unlikely, William stands up and moves over to the door, which he opens wide.

"I would like you to go now, Veronica, if you don't mind. I really need more time by myself to think things over."

There's a stony silence from Veronica who doesn't believe he means what he's saying. Minerva, whom I'm glad to see is not pining but looking very well, peers out through the bars of her cage, eyeing the open door with interest.

"Who rattled his cage?" she asks – and is ignored.

"Please just go," William repeats.

"I can't believe you're behaving like this!" Getting no reply, Veronica slowly picks up her coat and bag and walks towards the door. "So this is the end, is it, William?"

"Yes. I think it is."

Just for an instant, a look of genuine grief shows in her face, which suddenly looks more ivory-coloured than tanned. She stares straight ahead of her as she walks past him. Veronica may appear reasonably composed to William but she's having great difficulty holding back her tears.

He watches as she climbs into her car and slams the door shut. As it moves off down the drive, William leans against the wall, head back and eyes closed. He stays like this for several minutes. As soon as he reappears in the kitchen, Minerva pokes an inquiring beak out of her cage.

"Who rattled . . ."

"Shut up, you bloody fool!" says William, but his voice lacks any punch.

Chapter Ten

I'm feeling a bit ambivalent about William. I try and explain to Thomas.

"I'm *really* sorry that he's unhappy but it seems to me that he's now setting about making Veronica's life miserable."

"Does that matter to you? After all, she was the one whom you subjected to an attack by her cat and she was the one you pushed . . ."

"Yes, I know! There's no need to go on! How would you have felt if you'd just discovered your wife had been having a ten-year affair?"

"Girl, I had three wives and, as far as I know, they were all happy."

Thomas is laughing at me. I know he is.

"One wife after the other?"

"No, at the same time, actually."

"You must have been an unusual man, being able to keep three women contented. Did you bypass Limbo with that on your record?"

"No! I served my time. Very few of us avoid the interim period. Tell me, Kate. You say you're not sure what to think about William but I know you are worried that he is upset. Would you wish him to suffer more? Do you think that would be good for him?"

I know I must be 100% honest. Anyway, Thomas would see through any untruths.

"He did make life very hard for an awfully long time and it was he who drove Celia away." I feel suddenly angry. "He *hit* her, for Go . . ."

Thomas ignores my near faux pas. "I don't think you are all that ambivalent, Kate. You're still angry, aren't you?"

"Yes, I suppose I am."

I'm ashamed and I don't want Thomas to think badly of me. I have another stab at trying to explain how I'm feeling.

"The funny thing is, when I first found out about him and Veronica, I was more upset by her behaviour than his and now I'm feeling sorry for her and angry with him. It doesn't make any sense."

There's a pause and then he asks, "Do you think you will achieve anything by getting Celia to come home to her father?"

"You mean, there'd be no point, if William hasn't changed?"

"He has changed a little already. Did you ever hear him say that he felt guilty before?"

"I don't remember him saying he felt guilty about anything. I certainly never heard him say he was sorry. That hasn't changed."

There's another silence and I know that Thomas is

disappointed with me. I am disappointed at my lack of generosity.

Now I find myself back at the island and feeling a bit deflated. Thomas suggested that it would be a good idea for me to spend some time here and not to make plans for the future concerning Celia and William. He was very nice about it but he obviously thinks I need more of a cooling-off period before I can do anything useful. He reminded me that it might be a good idea not to try and rush things.

It's evening here and the air is still warm as I let myself descend towards the little house where I last saw Celia. Being dead is rather like being on holiday; I've lost all sense of time and I can't remember which day of the week it is. I think it's still September because I can see tractors with their trailers laden down with grapes, chugging along the dusty roads. If I'm remembering correctly, the *vendange* takes place towards the end of September.

Yes, because it was in September three years ago that Veronica surprised me by announcing she'd got airline tickets for a week away in France and I was to go with her.

"No argument! You look as though you need a break!" she'd said, plonking the tickets down on the table in front of me. "We'll have a great time, consume *vast* quantities of inexpensive plonk, eat mountains of delicious, garlic-ridden food and you will come back bronzed and beautiful – a new woman!"

"What about William?"

"William will be just fine! William will feed the parrot and walk the dog and look after the house."

91

"I'll have to ask him if he minds me disappearing for a whole week."

"Already done that and there's no problem."

"Are you sure?" I asked, still a little worried.

"I pointed out to him that he's always swanning off for weeks at a time, leaving you to keep everything on the rails and now you deserve a change of scene before you end up sounding like Minerva and with a waistline like Samson's."

"Thanks a lot!"

"That's what friends are for – to tell you the unpalatable truth! Your enemies – if you have any, which I very much doubt – wouldn't dream of telling you what you really need. They'd just sit back and discuss your shortcomings gleefully amongst themselves."

I was grateful for her generosity and we did have a good time. We stayed in a small house that belonged to friends of hers in a tiny village, perched on top of a hill. It was tucked away in the south-east corner of France, near the Spanish border. The area had apparently not yet been discovered by the hordes of tourists that thronged the beaches only twenty kilometres away.

There was a small supermarket, a *boulangerie*, two bars, a café, a church, the village square and thirty or so houses, all nudging shoulders in streets that were almost too narrow to drive a car in. There was also the all-important dusty, flat space in the shade of giant fig trees where the men met each evening to play boules and smoke.

One of the things I remember most about that week away was the scent of nicotiana. Its purple flowers were everywhere and when we sat out on the tiny balcony in the evening with our glasses full of milky *pastis*, the mingled perfumes of jasmine, lilies and nicotiana made us feel light-headed.

The night we arrived, I developed a bad migraine. I suppose it was from a mixture of flying, which I hate, and relief and excitement at just being away from William's ever-watchful eye. Veronica was perfect. She fed me the right painkillers, put me to bed and stayed quietly away from me until the next morning.

The week passed in a flash of sun, swimming, eating delicious food in unhygienic, dark, little restaurants and indulging ourselves in numerous wine-tasting sessions in the local inhabitants' garages. Everyone in the entire village seemed to be engaged in bottling their own wine and some of it was far from palatable. We hired a car and sneaked over the border, coming back with large quantities of glorious *Rioja*, which we hid under towels on the back seat. Then suddenly, it was time to go home.

I can tell that this island is not Mediterranean by the sound the sea is making, pounding the rocks in a nearby inlet. Light is shining out of an open downstairs window.

I know perfectly well that I can travel through bricks and concrete if necessary but when I do I still find myself shutting my eyes in case, this time, I'll end up splatted against a wall or, even worse, get stuck halfway through. So I tend to make for open doors and windows if they're around. It's hard to break the habits of a lifetime!

I approach the window and look in. Celia is sitting with her head in her hands. I can't make out if she's resting or if she's crying. As I get closer, I see there are the remains of tears on her cheeks and her eyes are red-rimmed. Her mind is full of thoughts of someone called Matt. Is that the name of a lover? I wonder. After all, she's twenty-six and pretty – if not quite at her best at the moment.

I'm amazed at the changes in her. When Celia left home, she was still very much a stocky schoolgirl. Now, she has a woman's build. I'm sad that she's cut her beautiful hair but she looks very striking, if tired, with the same scatter of freckles on her nose and cheeks but now her skin is a golden brown. I notice that her face is leaner than before and there are faint shadows under her marvellous blue eyes.

Why has she been crying? Is it because of this person called Matt? I slowly circle my daughter, taking in the fact that she's not wearing any rings. There's a small silver stud in the side of her nose, similar to the sort of decoration I've noticed being worn by some of the young ones around Dublin. She looks troubled. I so want to let her know that I'm here beside her. I want to be able to comfort her but even though I'm inches from her face, she doesn't seem the slightest bit aware of me. What would she do if she knew? Would she be frightened? Or does she still feel such contempt for her mother that she would tell me to go away and haunt someone else? I hope not.

Celia's sent only three postcards in over eight years. That would seem to indicate that she thinks she can manage without making any proper contact, that she's prepared to carry on her life without us. Has she been lonely? Has she suffered? I wonder, have there been times when she was tempted to pick up a phone and talk to us? To me, her life for eight long years is a complete blank.

I move very close to her and try whispering her name. No reaction! Then I let out a long, long sigh. Perhaps she will feel a change in temperature. Isn't that how ghostbusters know there's one around? Nothing. Not a flicker.

"Mama?"

I nearly jump out of my . . . ectoplasm?

A child's voice calls again from a nearby room.

"Mama!"

Celia gets up from the table and quickly leaves the room. I stay put, trying to come to terms with the fact that apparently my daughter is a mother! Why hadn't that possibility ever crossed my mind? For some reason, I know that she's not married. There are her ringless fingers for a start but there's something very solitary about her and as I look around the room, I can't see any signs of a man's presence in her life.

Good heavens! If Celia's a mother, that makes me a grandmother! Although I haven't got real knees – I feel decidedly weak in the general knee area.

Eventually, I follow her through the door and along a short passage. I can hear voices coming from a room at the far end. I stay just outside the door, suddenly overcome with nervousness at the thought of seeing my grandchild for the first time. Suddenly there's a loud crash, as though something has been thrown rather than dropped on to the floor. Then I hear my daughter speaking. It sounds as though she's finding it difficult to keep her voice low and contained.

"Matt! Calm down. Let me do it for you."

"No!" a child's voice cries. "No! Matt do it!"

There is the sound of hard objects being furiously shaken inside a container of some sort, then another crash.

"Matt do it! Matt do it!"

There's a silence, followed by the sound of sobbing.

Peering around the door, I see Celia picking up a plastic box and lid from the floor. There are cut-out shapes in the lid and I can see the pieces to fit the shapes are lying scattered over the rug beside the bed. A thin, dark-haired boy, who looks about six or seven, is sitting on the bed with knees drawn up under his chin and his arms wrapped tightly around them.

My heart gives a lurch. He's the spitting image of the young William in my mind-pictures. He has the same long, pointed face and dark eyes and that same look of vulnerability. His mind startles me. It's boiling over with anger and frustration.

Celia finishes picking up the plastic shapes and sits down on the bed beside her son.

"Matt? Let's do it together, shall we?"

He won't look at her but screws up his eyes and scowls. I move nearer to the foot of the bed to get a better look at him. Suddenly the child gives a cry and looks straight at me as though I were flesh and blood. His eyes are wide with fright. Celia, looking anxious, turns and stares in the same direction as he but I know she sees nothing.

"What is it?" she asks, in a worried voice, turning back to him.

But the boy has hidden his head in his hands.

I didn't mean to frighten the poor child. I didn't think for a moment that he would be aware of me – nobody else has reacted like that. I retreat from the room as fast as I can, forgetting all fear of solid objects, swooping up through ceiling, rafters and pantiled roof so fast I have difficulty stopping before getting tangled up in strands of low-lying cloud. Some sort of a braking system would come in handy in situations like this. Also a pair of stabilisers – like Celia had on her first bike – so that when I feel dizzy after a burst of excess speed, I won't think I'm about to keel over.

I get my breath back. It's all much more complicated than I thought it was going to be. No wonder Thomas told me not to rush things. *He* knew I had a grandchild and he must have known Matt would be able to see me. He might have warned me about there being something not quite right about the boy. I think I understand now why Celia was looking so drawn when I saw her sitting alone in the kitchen just a few minutes ago.

Chapter Eleven

It's morning and Thomas seems to have gone missing. I could do with a bit of help but there you are! He obviously feels that I should manage this next bit flying solo.

I can't help being pleased that Celia has made me a granny but how *could* she have not told me about the birth of her son? If she'd let me, I would have helped when I was alive but what use am I to either of them in my present condition?

It's really very hot up here and before I suffer from burn-off like clouds on a summer's morning, I think I'll go back down and see what's happening at the house.

Celia, wearing a large straw sun hat so I can't see her face, is weeding in the garden. She's stabbing at the soil with short, attacking movements. I can tell that she's trying her best to cope with feelings of worry, anger and despair. My daughter's doing exactly what I used to do when I was upset about something: going round in circles, getting more and more confused and exhausted and ending up further from finding a solution than when she started.

Matt's reaction to my invisible – as far as Celia's concerned – appearance the night before is bothering her. She's never seen him behave so strangely and is hoping that whatever caused it won't happen again. When she'd asked him to explain, he'd just shaken his head and started to curl a strand of his dark hair around his finger.

Celia's angry with herself because, earlier this morning, she shouted at Matt. The scene keeps replaying in her mind: Matt's fighting to get his shirt buttoned. His fingers seem to slip each time the edge of the button starts to go through the buttonhole. Celia tries to help but he pushes her away with his elbow. Frowning, she glances down at her watch.

"Matt, you've got to let me help you or you won't be ready for school in time."

Matt turns away from her so that he's facing the wall. He doesn't answer. His fingers are still fumbling helplessly with the wayward buttons. Celia watches him for a few moments longer. Suddenly, she can't bear to see him struggle any more. Grabbing hold of his arm, she spins him round to face her.

"For goodness' sake, let me do it or we'll be here all day!"

Matt tries to break away from her. He gives the same anguished cry I heard yesterday.

"No! Matt do it! Matt do it!"

"No!" insists his mother. "Stand still."

"Matt do it," he insists, wriggling like a worm.

Something snaps and before she can stop herself, Celia has slapped him hard on the arm. Matt bursts into tears and pulls away from her, throwing himself onto the floor in a corner of the room. Celia, full of remorse, goes over and kneels down beside him.

"Matt, I'm sorry. It's getting so late. I just wanted to help."

He jerks his head away, refusing to look at her.

For some time, she kneels beside him, trying to reason with him but Matt doesn't respond. He won't speak or even look at her; with head averted, he stares ahead of him at nothing.

Celia pauses, trowel in hand and gazes out towards the sea. How weary my daughter looks! She's thinking of the time her father hit her when she was the same age as Matt is now because she'd disobeyed him. I remember the occasion too. It was over something so trivial. She'd jumped over some shrubs I'd just planted and William told her not to do it again. When she thought he wasn't looking, she'd jumped them from the other direction but he'd seen her and been infuriated. He grabbed a nearby bamboo cane and hit her over the back of her legs with it. I remember the sharp intake of breath and the look of dislike on her face as she turned, determined not to cry in front of him, and walked away. Later on, he'd tried to make up. Celia wasn't having any of it and resorted to a surly silence that quickly made her father forget any feelings of regret he might have had earlier.

She always promised herself that if she ever had children of her own, she would never use any sort of physical force against them. Now, she's terrified that she's becoming like her father.

If only I could explain to her that what happened this morning wasn't such a dreadful crime; that being a parent is hell and trying to get it right all the time is even more hellish. I want to tell her I know how tired she is, how alone she feels, how concerned about her son. I want her to know that I understand.

I'm really feeling fed up with Thomas now! He made a very brief appearance a few minutes ago but was incredibly ambiguous when I said I didn't know what to do next.

"Girl, you can't expect me to *tell* you all the time what should be done," he said, in that marvellous voice of his that's so full of harmonics it's almost as if he's singing rather than talking to me. "You are here to learn and you will only learn if you listen, watch and then make up your own mind about what action to take, *if any*." The 'if any' was heavily stressed. "What is the matter with you? You have just found the missing two-thirds of your family and you're looking as miserable as sin!"

"Well, for starters, I had no idea that I'd become a granny and the very first time I see my grandson, apparently he could see me too and I succeeded in frightening the living daylights out of him."

Thomas gave one of his deep-throated chuckles.

"What did you expect? The poor child was already upset and then there he was, suddenly confronted by what is known down there as a ghost, peering at him from the bottom of his bed. Don't you remember what the average ghost story is like? Full of chilly-fingered wraiths, moaning and clanking their chains, bent on getting their own back on the unfortunate living. He's been watching too much television. That's all! I suggest that next time, you pick your moment a little more carefully."

"Oh, so you do think it's all right for me to try and get him used to the idea of having a dead granny who wants to drop in for the odd chat?"

"If you feel it is the right thing to do then you must do it," was all he would say, before doing his vanishing act again.

What on earth does he expect me to do? I wish he would be a little more specific! It's not as though I made such a marvellous job of being a mother to Celia all those years ago. I've a horrible feeling that I'll put my foot in it again and be even less successful, now that I'm dead. I don't know where to start if I'm to help her and Matt.

I wonder who Matt's father is and, more to the point, *where* he is. Celia must have become pregnant within the first year of leaving home – so he could be Irish, I suppose.

I was trying to get my thoughts in order just now when I felt a sort of pull – as though I were needed somewhere and my invisible cord that seems to keep me anchored to the world was being tugged. So I make my way down to the little house again, but carefully this time because I'm not sure if Matt's around.

Celia's talking on the phone or rather, shouting in a mixture of French and English. Unfortunately, my French is more or less non-existent so I can only follow a small part of the conversation. She eventually slams the phone down and bursts into tears.

"*Merde!*"

I *do* know what that means. It means that as well as being upset, she's extremely angry. From what I can gather, she's just asked someone called François for some money and he's said no. Matt's name came up several times during the argument. I wonder if this François could be the boy's father. He'd sounded as angry as she was and I could hear him yelling at her, saying that Matt was "*impossible*". I think he also said that he had no money.

With difficulty, I untangle some of my daughter's thoughts. It seems that there are problems at Matt's school; that he doesn't fit in and won't make any real effort to speak the language although he understands it well. He chooses to barely communicate in a muddled mixture of French and English. There are money problems too: Celia can't afford the specialist treatment he needs to help him improve his verbal and social skills. She's nearly come to the end of the small amount saved from teaching the flute during the summer holidays and she doesn't know whom to turn to for help. Oh, Lord! What a mess my poor daughter seems to have got herself into!

Suddenly, the tugging starts again and I find myself being drawn along the winding track to the road leading to the centre of the village. I see what looks like a small school with children playing outside in the yard. In one corner, there's a group of about seven or eight of them clustered around a child who is crouched on the ground like a hunted animal.

To my horror, I realise that it is Matt. His knees are bleeding and one of his shirtsleeves is torn. He's doing his best to block out the ring of jeering boys by holding his arms up in front of his face. My grandson's curled himself up, hedgehog-like, in a vain attempt at making himself look as small and insignificant as possible. He's not making a sound.

"*Pauvre p'tit Irlandais!*" A heavily built boy gives Matt a quick kick.

It's like watching a crowd at a lynching. I can feel the

mounting excitement of the group as they push closer to the child on the ground. More children run over and join the circle, curious to see what is happening. Their faces are eager, full of barely suppressed excitement. His very passivity seems to act as a catalyst. They're like hounds when they know their prey is wounded, that first blood has been drawn and it is only a matter of time before they move in for the kill.

There's apparently no teacher around to come to his aid but before I can do anything, Matt suddenly stumbles to his feet and lets out a highpitched scream that stops the others in their tracks. He pushes through them, arms flailing frantically. Then he breaks free from the clutching hands and runs towards the road with the pack in hot pursuit. Just as he rounds the boundary wall there is a bellow from behind them. An elderly man with white hair and thick glasses erupts into the yard, waving a cane. All of a sudden, the pursuit is called off and the boys reluctantly turn back towards the master.

I follow my grandson at a distance although I don't think he's in any sort of condition to be aware of me. His mind is full of thoughts of escape, of finding somewhere safe where he can hide. I expected him to turn towards home but he runs past the end of the lane and makes for the rocky beach near the lighthouse. He's panting and his breath is coming in short gasps as he scrambles through the rocks. Several times he falls and grazes himself but seems oblivious to pain. He leaves an untidy trail of small footprints in the sand. They zigzag around the rock pools and lead in a crooked line to the far end of the cove.

Finally, he stops at the base of a steep cliff. I watch him

as he clambers over the rocks and disappears into what looks like the entrance of a cave.

Very carefully, I make my way over to the dark gap in the rocks. Clumps of wild thyme and pink dianthus cling to the ledges and the sand here is covered in flotsam. I can feel a faint spray from the breaking waves. It tickles slightly as it travels through me. I pause at the cave's mouth, undecided. What if I have the same effect on Matt as I did last time? Then the sound of sobbing reaches me. I'm not going to hang around out here. I just have to do something. I go inside.

At first, I can hardly see him, after the brightness outside. As I get used to the dark, I can make out the boy's outline on the sand. He's lying, face downwards and his shoulders heave as he cries. I can't bear to see him like this and, Thomas or no Thomas, I have to do something to calm him down. If I kneel beside him and try not to loom at him from above and perhaps if I were on the far side so that he didn't feel cut off from making an escape, it would make him feel less threatened. I position myself between the back of the cave and my grandson. He still seems completely unaware of me. Very softly, I whisper his name.

"Matt!"

Immediately the sobbing stops. His whole body stiffens and his hands clench so tightly that his knuckles show up white in the gloomy light.

"Matt!" I repeat. "Don't be afraid. I'm your friend."

Slowly, he raises his head and turns to look straight at me. The pupils are so enlarged, his eyes seem almost completely black in the remains of the light from the cave's mouth. I can see that one false move on my part will make him take flight again.

"I want to help you, if you will let me. I've come all the way from Ireland to see you."

A flicker of recognition shows in his face.

"*Irlande?*" he says, pronouncing it the way the French do.

"Yes!" I say, with a smile. "Do you know about Ireland?"

"Mama comes from Irlande."

"I know."

Should I tell him that his mother is my daughter?

He takes me completely by surprise by suddenly saying, "Then you are my *grand-mère*."

He looks at me questioningly and I realise that he has access to my thoughts and, after the first couple of sentences, we've not been speaking out loud – we've been talking by thinking. Even his thoughts have a deliciously French sound to them. Also Matt seems unexpectedly fluent when he communicates in this way – unlike the inarticulate child I saw back at the house earlier on. I take a deep breath.

"Yes, I am your grandmother. My name is Kate."

He's sitting up now and has shed his look of alarm.

"*Bonjour, Grand-mère Kate!*" Then he leans forward to see me more clearly. "Are you a *fantôme?*"

I have to make a clean breast of it. There's no point in pretending now because it will only lead to problems later on. After all, I *am* dead. I just hope that by admitting I'm a ghost I won't upset him all over again.

"A phantom? Yes, I suppose I am although we usually call someone like me a ghost or a spirit."

Matt's reaction is surprisingly sanguine. He nods.

"I thought you were . . . a ghost." He's suddenly overcome by a small boy's inquisitiveness. "Can I put my hand through you?"

I feel slightly taken aback by his question and I'm not sure that I quite like the idea of being poked at by an inquiring finger. Still, I'd better not spoil things when we seem to be making such good progress. I give a nod and hope it won't be too unpleasant.

"OK! You can if you want."

Matt gets to his feet with a look of nervous anticipation. He suddenly darts forward and makes several quick swiping movements with his arm as if he were intent on winning points in a fencing tournament. It feels a little peculiar, this being sliced in two by an invisible rapier but nothing I can't handle. After all, what about my ability to osmose through walls etc?

"*Fantastique!*" he exclaims, his face now wreathed in an enormous smile.

I realise that this is the first time I've seen him smile. I know I probably sound like a typical fond granny – but he looks just gorgeous!

Chapter Twelve

It's a funny thing but Matt seems to accept the fact that I'm his dead grandmother without turning a hair. We spent nearly an hour together this afternoon, sometimes talking out loud, mostly just communicating through thought. Celia has obviously told him a little about her old home. I filled in some of the gaps, telling him about Sam's son being given the name, Samson – which he thought was hilarious. But the thing that fascinated Matt most was the idea of a parrot called Minerva.

"You have a *parrot*?" he asked.

"Yes, I have, or rather, I had a parrot. She's still there with your grandfather but she uses bad language and that makes him cross."

An expression of pleasure appeared on his face.

"What does she say?"

"Rude things! I'd better not tell you. Not the sort of things that you would say anyway."

"Oh, I can swear in French and English. Shall I tell you some of the words I know?" he asked, eagerly.

"I don't think your mother would approve."

"She uses swear words sometimes." He looked at me thoughtfully. "Would Mama mind me being here with you?"

"I'm not sure, Matt. She can't see or hear me like you can."

"She might be frightened if she knew I had a friend who is a ghost."

"Yes," I replied, "she might be a little surprised."

"Well, I don't think I shall tell her. You *are* my secret, *Grand-mère* Kate."

"Do you think it's a good idea to keep secrets from her?"

"*She* has secrets. She won't tell me about lots of things."

"Well, perhaps I can be your secret for now," I said, carefully.

Later on, I finally managed to get him to talk about what had happened earlier in the schoolyard.

"Why were they doing that to you?" I asked him.

"Because they don't like me."

"Why on earth don't they like you?"

There was a moment's silence and then he said in a strangely adult voice, *"Parce-que, je suis différent."*

"Because you are different?"

"Yes."

"How are you different from them, Matt?"

"I don't sound like them and . . ."

"Yes?"

He looked towards the cave entrance and the sunlit world outside, pursing his lips tightly together before continuing.

". . . and I don't have a proper father. He does not like me. They call me *un bâtard*. I don't know what that word is in English. Do you know what it means, *Grand-mère Kate*?"

"Yes, I know the word but it's meaningless, Matt." I

looked straight at him, forcing him to meet my eye. "It has *no* meaning at all. Just because your mother chose not to marry your father does not make the slightest bit of difference to who or what you are. You are Matt and that's good enough for me – and they're stupid if they can't understand that."

"But they say that it is a terrible thing and because I have not been baptised a Catholic I am damned and will burn forever."

The memory of Celia in tears, as a result of the cruel taunting all those years ago and now the same thing with Matt, made me want to shout with anger. Thomas! If you are anywhere around, tell me why are people still so pig-ignorant, so unkind? Why do they pass on to their children their own wretched hang-ups and narrow-mindedness?

No answer! He must be busy somewhere or else he thinks it's a daft question.

Matt took quite a bit of persuading that I had it on higher authority that burning forever was not on the cards. He was full of 'Didier says . . .' or 'But Claude told me . . .' In the end, he had to accept that my being dead meant that I was probably more likely to have a better possession of the facts than either young Didier or Claude. I'm glad he doesn't know how unclear an awful lot of it still is to me. He was rather sceptical though when I said I hadn't personally met God.

"But you said you were dead so you *must* have seen him."

"It doesn't seem to be quite as easy as that I'm afraid, Matt. You'll just have to trust me when I tell you that you will not, I repeat not, burn forever after you die. Honestly!"

He looked a bit brighter when I explained that I had my own guardian angel who was helping me sort things out. I didn't tell him that Thomas kept leaving me in the lurch when I thought I most needed his support and guidance.

The thing that really cheered him up though was when he asked if I could help him 'make the others behave'.

"Would you do something, *Grand-mère Kate?*" he asked in his lightly accented voice.

"What sort of thing were you thinking of?" I asked, cautiously.

With a gleam in his eye, he said, "Nothing to really hurt them but could you frighten them *un petit peu* . . . just a little?"

I found myself wondering what Thomas would think about the direction the conversation was taking but the angelic airwaves didn't seem to be open. To be honest, nothing would have given me greater pleasure than to push the ringleaders over the top of the cliff above us.

I said, "If you go home now and then tomorrow go to school as normal, I will see what I can do to help." A sudden thought occurred to me, "You won't tell anyone about me at school, will you, Matt?"

His voice sounded scornful. "Of *course* not!" Then he added, "I'm very good at keeping secrets, you know."

An early morning sun is shining across the small fields. It casts long shadows of trees and houses onto the bracken and dried-up grasses. Even though it is the end of September, there's heat in its rays. I can see tiny wisps of dew curling up into the air like miniature smoke signals as it warms the petals and leaves of plants and flowers.

I've noticed that I can see things in much more detail than when I was alive and colours are so vivid that they seem to hum at different frequencies. Red and orange sound particularly jazzy and when the two meet in the petals of the same flower, the resulting syncopation is really quite something!

One of the other things I've realised is that most animals, unless they're particularly short-sighted and stupid, and all birds can see me. I've had a few near misses with some of the faster-flying ones and one or two that refused to change their flight path. Before I could take evasive action, they'd barrelled their way straight through me, leaving me feeling like a rather insubstantial slice of Gruyère cheese. Most of them however are very obliging. I do have to watch out for anything sleeping on the wing though because I find they tend to get sidetracked into my air corridor.

Yesterday, after Matt left me and I was spiralling gently up into the clouds, I found that a cluster of rather dopey martins had changed course in their sleep and had joined me on my climb. I had to point each bird in the right direction – at least I hope it was the right direction – and give quite a vigorous puff to send it on its way again.

I've also noticed that there are quite a few of my sort floating around. You know, ghosts, spirits – whatever. Not that they take much notice of me or of each other. Everyone seems as though they have too much to do to waste any time swapping observations on life in Limbo. I suppose that everyone's Limbo is different. Anyway, most of them steam around with a look of puzzled concentration. I expect that's how I look at the moment too.

Thomas is still not broadcasting so I don't know if he's

away or just watching and saying nothing. Well, if that's how he wants to play it, fine! But I'm not going to drift about the place doing nothing. Perhaps it's a good thing if he's not around because I've thought up some good ways of sorting out Matt's little problem and I want to get down to business without any prolonged discussions on the methods I intend using.

It's lovely and warm on the roof and I must have dozed off! While I waited for my grandson to appear, I stretched out over the tiles so that I wasn't quite touching but could feel the little eddies of warm air rising from between their curved surfaces. It's a bit like a hot-air Jacuzzi; it tickles and massages you in unexpected places!

I've suddenly woken up to find Matt staring at me from the front garden with a look of entreaty. Celia's walking towards the laneway and is thinking about the man called François. Her thoughts are not happy ones.

"*Grand-mère Kate*! Please wake up!" Matt begs, silently so that his mother won't hear. "I thought I would have to throw my football at you to wake you!"

"I'm extremely glad you didn't," I reply, slowly floating down beside him. "It would be rather like being a skittle in a bowling alley. You can't chuck balls at me, you know. You have to learn to treat dead grandmothers with respect!"

He gives me one of his rare smiles.

"Matt! What on *earth* are you smiling at?" asks Celia, looking over at him with a puzzled expression.

The smile vanishes. Matt hangs his head and says nothing.

Celia gives a small shrug of irritation and continues walking.

"Just hurry up or you'll be late for school . . . again."

He dawdles after her, head still down. I manage to give him a little nudge and remind him that today is payback day. His chin comes up and his step quickens.

I've been practising nudging during the times when my mind is overheated from thinking and worrying. It was quite difficult at first but I've also started to be able to move objects around a little and I'm even getting adept at lifting quite heavy things off the ground for up to half a minute at a time. I must have been given these abilities for some reason – so I might as well work at them – and put them to good use – when I get the chance.

Matt says goodbye to Celia at the school gate and watches her as she walks down the road, shopping basket over her arm. Her shoulders look slightly hunched and I can feel the tension in the muscles of her neck and back.

As soon as he sees the coast is clear, Matt turns and looks at me. There's no one else in the yard and I can hear a terrific racket coming from within the building. Obviously adult supervision is non-existent or else the teacher or teachers haven't yet arrived.

"Are you coming in, *Grand-mère Kate?*"

"No, Matt. I will wait for you outside and I will be ready for them when you have your morning break." Seeing the anxious look on his face, I add, "When the teacher comes, you go in too. They won't do anything when he's in the room, will they?"

"No," he says, in a small, rather doubtful voice.

At that moment, the elderly man I had seen yesterday walks into the schoolyard, polishing his glasses with a none too clean handkerchief. He holds them at arm's length and peers at them before putting them back on his nose. He glances over at Matt who hurriedly disappears into the building.

Time passes quite quickly as I practise my nudging, sliding and lifting skills. Very soon, children begin to straggle out into the yard and among them, comes a hesitant-looking Matt.

Within just a few minutes, the bullying begins. It's easy to see who are the ringleaders: the heavily built boy who kicked Matt yesterday and a tall, pale creature with a spotty face and shifty eyes. They both look two or three years older than my slightly built grandson. They isolate Matt from the others by pushing him into a corner. Before they can get properly into their stride, I position myself between the two boys. Although I can't understand exactly what they're thinking, it's easy to anticipate their actions. I know I told Matt that, generally, violence was not a good idea but I can't help feeling that these two lads wouldn't understand anything that didn't cause just a little pain. I go into action.

Suddenly, the short one draws back his right foot and . . . goodness me! He lands a hefty wallop on the shins of the tall one, who lets out a yell of indignation. The short one is looking down at his foot as if it belonged to someone else. It does. To me! The short one is looking as surprised as the tall one.

There's a ferocious stream of abuse from the wounded party who then finds his left fist has made contact with his partner-in-crime's jaw. Another angry shout but this time from the short one, who clutches his face while the tall one sucks at his knuckles.

The air is riddled with invective. Perhaps it's just as well I can't translate it but I'm certainly getting the general drift. The three boys suddenly find themselves the centre of attention as all the children gather round to get a better glimpse of the action.

Matt takes a step nearer and, after darting a quick glance at me, stands looking up at them. Suddenly he points to a large clump of dandelion leaves growing in a crack in the wall. He looks steadfastly at the short one. The boy immediately goes over, tears off a handful of leaves, stuffs them into his mouth and starts to slowly chew. He looks rather like a thoughtful cow that has bitten off too big a mouthful of greenery. There are stifled giggles from the watching children. Then Matt turns his attention to the tall one who suddenly bends down and picks up a handful of grit and dust. He starts to wipe it slowly and carefully into his cheeks, chin and forehead. The resulting effect is of some rather inexpertly painted lanky warrior. More delighted giggles.

Matt surveys them for a brief moment and then he turns and walks away to the sound of laughter and cheering, especially from some of the younger members of the audience. They seem to be thoroughly enjoying the sight of the two bullies, who are now sitting on the dirty ground, looking dazed and discomforted. Three or four of the children are clustered around Matt, full of praise and obviously impressed by his sudden sangfroid in the face of uneven odds.

I'm just moving in for the grand finale when I am halted by Thomas's voice.

"Take it easy, girl! Don't overdo it."

"But I was just going to put the finishing touches to the whole thing," I remonstrate, rather crossly. What did he think I'd done all that practising for? "Why did you have to pick this precise moment to grace us with your presence?" I stop, appalled. I wouldn't have dreamed of talking to Thomas like that a few days ago and I'm immediately contrite. "I'm sorry, Thomas. That was rude of me. I was just so caught up in what was happening to Matt and you've been missing for quite a while."

"That's perfectly all right but 'enough is enough' as they say!"

"Quite! But will it be enough to keep those two in order, I wonder?"

"For the moment, yes. You've given them something to think about but I think that levitation, bi-location and shape-shifting and all that sort of thing would be just a little over the top. Don't you?"

"What about all that stuff in the Bible about sending down plagues of locusts and boils and crop failures? Wasn't that rather melodramatic and . . . vengeful?"

Thomas laughs. A big, deep-chested laugh. It's a little like unexpected thunder from unseen clouds on a summer's day.

"When you lived down there, did you believe everything you read in the papers?"

"Of course not."

"Well? Do you think *He* would waste his time with that sort of a carry-on? Mother Nature can be quite cantankerous sometimes, you know."

"Sorry! I was being stupid," I apologise.

And then, as suddenly as he had come, he was gone

117

again, leaving me with a faint crackle of static in my ears.

I think, judging from the cheerful expression on Matt's face last time I looked, it's probably all right if I leave for a little while too.

Chapter Thirteen

I'm getting that feeling again of being pulled. Before I've had time to think, I find myself changing direction and suddenly I'm back in Ireland. As far as I can make out, Thomas is not with me but I'm sure it was he who decided that I should be here.

I'm in the kitchen at home and an exasperated-looking William has just let Veronica in the door. As he closes the door, he puts something in his pocket. It looked like a postcard. He takes a deep breath before looking straight at her. I can see that something other than Veronica's arrival has upset him badly.

"Well? Why have you come back? I thought we'd come to an understanding."

"No, William. *You* thought we had. You made up your mind that our relationship was a bad thing and it was *you* who decided that we shouldn't meet again. I've given this a lot of thought and I don't want to walk away."

I'm astonished. I've never heard Veronica sound or look so serious before.

"I know you're feeling guilty about the fact that we had an affair while Kate was alive but that's no reason to turn your back on me now. If it makes you feel any better, since we last talked, I've found it harder to reconcile what we did too. I *know* it was wrong and I'm sorry... sorry that I can't make it up to her... sorry that I lied to her."

This new woman, who speaks in a low voice but with a sense of urgency, is like a stranger to me. William too is looking surprised. He stands very still, hands by his side. He doesn't know quite how to respond to a subdued Veronica. In the past, it was difficult to get a word in edgeways when she was around. She fired words into the air as easily as she flung herself physically into spontaneous embraces or extravagant gestures, never giving a thought to whether her actions were appropriate or not. Now, she makes no move towards him, as though she's afraid to invade his space. From her thoughts I can see that she's terrified of making the wrong move, of doing anything that will make William send her away again. She waits patiently for him to answer her.

Seeing that it's up to him to say something, he clears his throat almost nervously and then runs his fingers through his hair in the way I remember so well.

"You've caught me a little off-balance, I'm afraid. I wasn't expecting you." William's looking unwell. He's lost weight and the skin under his eyes is puffy. He looks like a man who can't sleep and whose waking thoughts trouble him deeply. "I always got the impression that you never *really* cared for me – that our relationship lasted as long as it did out of habit rather than because of any real sense of commitment. What has brought about this change of heart?" he asks, puzzled.

"I'm not sure really. It's just that since Kate died, I've had four weeks to think about things and I realise now, William, that I really do love you." Veronica sounds almost as though she's surprised at what she has just said.

I can't believe that I've been gone that long! I also find it difficult to equate Veronica declaring her love to William with the woman who told me that she had no intention of ever allowing herself to be hurt by falling in love again.

I drift down into the corner near Minerva's cage. The stupid bird's yanked out more of her feathers and is looking really terrible. She's watching Veronica and William with a morose expression. I'd forgotten that I would be visible to her and, as soon as I land, she gives out this appalling screech that makes the pair of them nearly jump out of their skins. Then she claws her way across the bars towards me where she stops, head tilted to one side, black beady eye looking straight at me.

"Bugger, bugger, bugger!" she screams in welcome.

"Bloody bird," comments William, automatically.

"What on earth did she do *that* for?" asks Veronica, peering straight through me. "Why's Minerva staring at the corner of the room like that? There's nothing there but she looks as though she thinks there is."

"She's mad, that's all! Katherine maintained Minerva was deeply traumatised by being snatched from the jungle and transported halfway across the world in a wooden crate to go and live with a foul-mouthed family who then dumped her in a badly run zoo. She said it was no surprise to her that the wretched creature tore out her feathers and swore."

Minerva's now on her perch, doing a sort of mad two-step routine which involves shifting her weight from one foot to the other while bobbing her head up and down. William's looking at her strangely.

"That's very odd!"

"Why?"

"The only person Minerva ever did that for was Katherine."

"Perhaps she's missing her and is thinking about her," suggests Veronica, rather lamely.

For a moment, William sounds like his old self and his voice is tinged with sarcasm, "And I suppose Minerva's deeply disturbed because it's you and not Katherine who's just walked in the door."

This is not getting anyone anywhere. I give Minerva a long, hard look before taking a shortcut through the end wall into the garden. In the background, I hear her as she, undaunted, restarts her mantra.

"Well, I'll be bug . . ."

"Shut up!" William shouts.

She counters with a quick, "Who rattled *his* cage?"

Minerva always liked to have the last word.

It's damp and autumnal out here and everything is dripping from an earlier shower. My poor garden is in a mess, with uncut grass and fruit rotting on the ground. The young eucalyptus by the gate is leaning at an even more noticeable angle and one of the old birch trees has lost a branch the width of a man's thigh. A great jagged tear blackens the papery trunk.

Why is William letting it all go to rack and ruin? It's as if he can't summon up enough energy to make an effort in any direction at the moment. Especially not in the area of his relationship with Veronica. I hate to see him so deflated – and her so unsure.

I wander around the vegetable garden that now has more weeds than vegetables in it. Then I look over to the other side of the valley where the deer are moving across the mountain, white rumps gleaming in the early evening dark. I see pale shreds of mist creeping up the field from the river and in the whiteness, I can just make out a solitary figure. I know, even from this distance, that it's not someone from the living world.

I visit some of the places along the water's edge where I used to take Celia when she was small; our favourite bend, where we once saw otters playing, sliding in the mud and diving into the river. They turned and twisted, suddenly breaking the surface of the peat-brown water with fur sleeked backed on their heads to repeat the game all over again. We watched them for ages, Celia so full of pleasure at the unexpected sight she was lost for words.

I laugh to myself when I remember how, at the next bend, we'd once sat down on the grass bank, only to jump up a few minutes later. We'd chosen a red ants' nest on which to rest. The only cure was to rip off our knickers and dip our backsides into the icy cold water. Luckily, none of the local sheep farmers were around to be scandalised.

I remember the time Celia, aged six or so, had run back to me on one of our walks, her face chalk-white.

"You've got to come!" she gasped, pulling at my hand.

"What is it? What's the matter?"

"Come! Please come."

I'd followed her, stumbling through the low hanging

branches of the pines. Even though her legs were scratched and bleeding, she fought her way on, through the narrow belt of trees to the other side. Hanging from the double strands of barbed wire forestry fence was a hind. She'd died a little while before and was still warm to the touch. Her back leg had caught in the wire where she'd jumped in a frantic attempt to get away from a poacher. She'd been wounded in the neck, not badly enough to kill her outright, sometime during the previous night. Celia begged me to do something.

"Make her all right, Mummy."

"I can't, darling. She's dead."

"No! You can make her better. You can!"

It had taken some time to persuade her that I could do nothing for the deer. Finally, giving up on me, Celia had looked once more into the dark, unseeing eyes and walked away.

She didn't talk all the way back to the house. I remember thinking that another chunk of innocence had been obliterated and yet another step taken towards the uncomfortable business of adulthood. I remember thinking too that in Celia's eyes I'd let her down – again.

I must have spent a long time outside in the darkness, remembering. I suddenly think of William. There's something different about him – and Veronica too. Is it possible that my death had been the catalyst that was needed to help them both rethink ideas that had become fixed? It's just dawned on me that all the anger I felt over their relationship has been extinguished, snuffed out like a candle flame.

I feel nervous about going back to the house. If Veronica has stayed, it would be like snooping on my part. But if she's left and William is on his own, I'd like to make sure that he's all right. That's if I can avoid being spotted by Minerva. Perhaps I could give her a little pep-talk and tell her she's not to make it so obvious when she knows I'm around.

Poor old Samson! I suppose it's a good thing that he's not here too. That would really complicate matters. If he wagged his tail and looked pleased to see me as well as Minerva doing her welcome routine, William would really start to think he was losing the plot.

Very carefully, I ease myself through the window at the opposite end of the kitchen to the parrot's cage. The fridge blocks her view in this direction so I should be safe. They're both there, sitting, one at each side of the table, drinking coffee. Veronica is dying to have a cigarette but has managed to hold back. She knows how much William hates the way the smell of smoke clings to his hair and clothes and how its staleness lingers in the room the following day. I see from the clock on the wall that it's past midnight.

William is talking in a tired voice. A card with a French stamp is lying on the table in front of him.

"The thing is, it's the first time Celia has sent a postcard with her address and so it's the first opportunity I've had to write to her in eight years. It's hard enough to write anything after all this time, especially considering the way things were when she left. If I get in touch now, how on earth do I tell her that her mother's dead?"

"You can't keep it from her, William. She has to be told."

"With Kate gone, there would be no reason for her to

125

come back. I very much doubt that her feelings towards me have changed."

That's the first time I've heard my husband call me Kate and not Katherine. I wonder why he did. What's the significance?

"I thought that Kate told me you refused to let her look for Celia. She thought you'd washed your hands of her."

"I allowed my wife to think a lot of things about me that weren't true."

"Why?"

"I don't know – some sort of fatal lethargy? I very quickly realised I'd made a bad mistake in marrying her but I didn't seem to be able to summon up the mental energy to talk it all through. It seemed somehow kinder not to tell her the truth. That way, she could believe there was always the possibility that things might improve between us."

"She said that she felt you were determined not to ever let her see the real you; almost as if you were hiding something."

"Perhaps because I was too ashamed to let her know who the 'real me' was." William closes his eyes for a moment and I can feel that his mind is full of regret and an awful sense of hopelessness. "I was a bad husband and an even worse father but I can't undo all that history. Now, I suppose, I want to erase all the mistakes, the way footmarks are wiped out by the incoming tide, and be given a second chance."

Veronica suddenly sits up and protests.

"Don't be silly, William! Kate was a dear but she wasn't the right woman for you. She lacked any sort of ambition and she let you walk all over her – and that wasn't good for you."

William gives a small, wry smile. She continues, leaning forward towards him over the table and speaking vehemently.

"You didn't beat her. You weren't a raving alcoholic and you gave her a lovely home to live in and an attractive daughter. All right, so Celia left home in a huff! She's not the only kid in the world to do that. The fact remains that however angry she was, she *has* got in touch. Don't be so negative! Sorry if you think I'm being blunt. It's got to be said and it seems that I'm the only one who's prepared to talk to you in a straightforward way. Apart from Minerva, that is!"

She gives him an encouraging smile but William is still looking bleak.

I find it rather comforting to hear Veronica sounding more like her old self again – and she's right. I wasn't the ideal woman for William. I wonder how well she really knows him though. She may be closer to him than I ever managed to get but has he told her about that man Joseph or about his prodigal parents? I somehow don't think he has.

Veronica leans back in her chair and then says something that would make my hair stand on end, if I had any.

"Of course, you know that you weren't the only one to be unfaithful."

William slowly lowers his coffee cup and stares at her.

"What did you just say?"

"Kate had a fling when you were away on one of your lecture junkets."

"Rubbish! She would never have done any such thing."

"On the contrary, my dearest William. It was the summer after Celia left. Kate never told me about it but I saw her with a man one day when I came up to the house when she wasn't expecting me. By the way they behaved towards each other, I knew straight away they were lovers. I never let her know that I'd seen them though."

William's expression changes from disbelief to one of anger.

"How could she? Did you know who he was?"

"No. He was very young though and rather dishy. I didn't manage to get a proper look but I thought he seemed rather nice."

"Oh, did you?" William's breathing heavily. It's obvious that he feels he's been hit on the back of the head with a sledgehammer. "And you never thought to tell me?"

Veronica looks at him and starts to laugh.

"You're quite amazing! Why on earth should I have told you? Did either you or I tell Kate about us?"

Good point! I think to myself. That stops William in his tracks for a moment. Then he rallies.

"But she somehow always managed to give off the aura of being hard done by – as if she were the only virtuous one."

"I think Kate *was* virtuous; with that one exception. Think, William! She knew that you didn't really love her. Her one and only child had done a disappearing act a few months earlier. You were either away or buried in your latest book. She must have felt terribly lonely. She wasn't a grumbler, you know. Most of the time she was incredibly loyal to you but she *was* human. Perhaps that young man made her happy for a little while. Would you deny that

128

she'd the right to have a little bit of pleasure in her life?"

William sits silently for a while before answering her. What he says next surprises me. This conversation is turning out to be full of them.

"I've been extraordinarily selfish, haven't I?"

"I think we both have but I'm not going to weep about it ad infinitum. William, you're not as young as you were and even I'm beginning to show signs of wear and tear. One can't be a siren forever! Any more than one can spend what remains of a life in grieving. Come on! Cheer up! It's not all bad, you know." Veronica gets up and goes round to his side of the table and gives him a quick kiss on the cheek. "Right! It's late and I've an important meeting with impossible clients in the morning. I mustn't go in looking too much like a witch." She picks up her jacket from the chair. "Keep in touch and . . . go to bed, for heaven's sake. You look like death warmed up!"

Then she's gone, closing the door behind her with a click. I can hear her high heels on the paving stones outside as she walks briskly to her car. You have to hand it to Veronica. Underneath all the make-up and haute couture, she's funny and a lot more courageous than I realised. She could never be accused of being a wimp.

I feel strangely relieved that she's told my husband about Milo. I'm also happy that she's taking William in hand and I admire the way she seems to be able to keep an eye on him without making him feel threatened or crowded. Would that I had had a little more of Veronica's sophistication and been a little less of an innocent!

It's a bit late to moan about it now, though and she doesn't have it all her own way. She'd get a bit of a surprise if she could see me in my non-dimensional present state! No doubt, once she was over the shock, my friend would have something outrageous to say – something along the lines of: 'Love the floaty drapes. Kate dear, believe me, the new you is a vast improvement on the old one!' Perhaps it is!

Chapter Fourteen

"Are you feeling all right, Kate?" Thomas's voice breaks into my thoughts.

"Oh, you're back! Yes, I'm fine. I was just wondering where the best place is for me to be at the moment. Should I try and find a way to encourage William to write to Celia or should I go back to her and Matt and see what's going on there?"

"Do you see a change in William?"

"Yes, I do. A big change."

"Don't you think you should trust him to make up his own mind in his own time?"

"I suppose so but don't ask me to leave the other two to make up their minds. Celia's so full of worry she can't think straight and Matt doesn't know whether he's coming or going. He's so mixed up in his head. What *is* wrong with him, Thomas? He has absolutely no trouble at all making himself understood when he's communicating with me. I know he's very bright but what stops him from behaving like a normal seven-year-old with other people for the rest of the time? Is he autistic, dyslexic?"

"There you go! Just like the rest of them down there! You're trying to put a label on the boy. What good does that do?"

"It's all very well you saying that but down there you don't get the right treatment if they can't give a name to what's wrong with you. Mind you, even when they do have a name for it, that doesn't automatically mean that the treatment you end up getting is the right one. There's something wrong with him. I suppose what I want to know is, will it be possible at some stage for Matt to be more normal – more like other boys of his age?"

"Like Didier and Claude, you mean?"

"Of course not like them!"

"A lot of people would consider them to represent what passes for normal."

"You know what I mean," I say, resentful that he doesn't seem to be taking Matt's situation seriously enough.

"Girl, you worry too much. I think that the experts down there would find a label for Matt quite easily but you would be surprised what a little love and understanding and being in the right environment does for a boy like him. Have you considered what harm it does to a child to have his father turn away from him and for his mother to be so unhappy? No wonder poor Matt is angry and confused."

"Well, I don't think he is in the right environment at the moment."

"Perhaps not," says Thomas.

"Do you mind if I go back there then?"

"No, Kate. I don't mind, but be careful. Can I make a suggestion?"

"Of course."

"I've said it before. Don't rush into anything. Look and listen before you make up your mind. You can be a tad impulsive sometimes!"

I close my eyes and concentrate on Celia and Matt.

Matt's angry. The air around him is vibrating with his anger. He's so absorbed in how he feels, he doesn't see me at first. He's sitting on the floor of his bedroom with one canvas shoe off and one on. He's attempting to tie the lace of the shoe he's wearing. Each time he winds the lace around his finger, it seems to take on a life of its own and slips from his grasp. He's swearing in his head, repeating the word his mother used on the phone when she talked to François a few days earlier.

"*Merde! Oh, merde!*"

"Hello, Matt! You seem to have a problem."

He jumps and looks guilty.

"*Oh, bonjour, Grand-mère Kate!* I can't do the lace up. It doesn't do what I want."

"I said you had a problem, Matt but it's only a very little problem. Let's see if you can do it up with my help."

So we spend the next half an hour with me helping him. Gradually I help less and less and finally he manages on his own.

"Well done! You did it all by yourself that time. I wasn't helping the least little bit but you did it!" The enormous smile on Matt's face is like the sun coming out after a cloudy day that had threatened squally showers. "Next time you find yourself getting angry, just remember that *you* have to be the one to help the lace be tied or the button done up and then you'll find it easy."

I look around the room for clues to tell me what my grandson is interested in. On a table under the window are some watercolour paints, brushes and pieces of paper.

"Do you like painting, Matt?"

He nods vigorously.

"Mama has all my paintings in a big box. She says I'm very good for my age."

"Would you paint something for me?" A thought suddenly occurs to me. "If I described my house – the house where your mother grew up, would you paint it for me?"

Without answering, he jumps up and almost runs to the table, still wearing one shoe. Grabbing a paintbrush, Matt dips it in a yoghurt pot of water and looks at me expectantly.

"Go on, *Grand-mère Kate!* I am ready."

I carefully describe the house; the way the larch trees stand over one gable end, their golden needles carpeting the stone path below. I tell him how the crimson creeper has almost completely covered the original white-washed walls and climbed into the gutter and started its ascent of the grey slate roof. I tell him the number of windows in the front and how, if you look carefully, you can see Minerva sitting on her perch in the sunshine in one of the kitchen windows. I show him which green to choose to paint in the garden door and how there is a white rose that climbs an old apple tree in between the door and the first window on the right. I describe how the forest nearly surrounds the house on three sides and that, when you walk up the garden towards the house, you can see the spiky tops of the trees beyond. Behind them, I tell him, stand the purple and grey-blue mountains.

He paints quickly and deftly and he's good. Very good! When he's finished, I'm amazed at how close the likeness is to the house in the glen. Surely, when Celia sees this, it will make her want to go home?

What I hadn't reckoned on was that she might not have had any means of showing him with a photograph what the place was like. I'd been sure she'd have taken something with her when she left all those years ago. Apparently not!

When Matt rushes into the kitchen to show her his latest work of art, Celia's in the middle of preparing a meal and barely glances up when he erupts into the room.

"Matt! Why are you wearing one shoe? Go and put the other one on!"

She sounds irritable. I want to shake her. Her son, my grandson has just painted the most amazing picture and she's chopping onions and being grumpy. But Matt doesn't give up easily.

"Mama! This is a picture of your home in *Irlande*."

He pushes the painting in front of her and she pauses, knife in mid-cut. Her eyes widen as she takes in the picture her son holds in hands that tremble with excitement.

"Is it good, Mama?"

When Celia speaks, she sounds puzzled, almost alarmed.

"How did you know that it looked like that?" She turns to him, frowning. "You've never seen the house. How could you know what it looked like?"

Matt, suddenly smelling danger, comes up with an inspired solution.

"Matt's dream. The house was in Matt's dream."

"How did you know it was the house where I used to live?"

"Matt knows," is all he will say.

When Celia tries to persist in her questioning, the hangdog look comes back and he clams up completely. Oh, dear! Well done, Kate! I didn't take the advice Thomas gave me, yet again, but I was so sure she'd at least have talked about how the house was. Instead of my daughter being reminded of her old home and her starting to think that perhaps it's time to go back, I've made her feel even more unsettled. Worst of all, I've been responsible for Matt getting upset again. Apparently, grandmotherhood is not easy – even if you are an invisible one.

Back in his bedroom, Matt drops the painting on the table and turns to me dejectedly.

"Why wasn't she pleased with my picture? You said that it was just like the real house."

How much should I tell him? He already knows that his grandmother is dead. Presumably, Celia still thinks I'm alive and well. Although I wonder why she's left it until now to send her address home. Is it because she's too proud to admit she's in trouble and is hoping we'll ask her to come back first? That must be it! She's waiting for us to make the first move.

I look into my grandson's troubled eyes and my heart sinks. He thinks, that because I'm a ghost, I can make miracles happen.

"Why do you get so angry with yourself, Matt? And why won't you talk to people sometimes?" He leans against the wall, gazing out of the window through a fringe of black hair and, almost as if to prove the point, doesn't answer. I move closer to him. "I told you who I was and no one else knows about me – only you. Don't you think you could explain a little bit about who *you* are to me? I really would like to understand better. I'm so happy to find that I have a grandson but I don't know very much about you."

He considers what I've said for a few moments and then replies in a subdued voice, "I told you in the cave, *Grand-mère Kate*. I am different. Not just because I am not French. I can't do some of the things in class that the others do and when I look at words, I get muddled up and they don't make any sense. *Le Prof* says that I am stupid."

"But you know that's not true, don't you?"

"I think I *am* stupid or I would be able to read like them."

"Can they paint like you, Matt?"

After a pause he says, "No."

"Did any of the others see me when I was in the playground with you and Claude and Didier?"

Again, that lovely, fugitive grin. "No!"

"Well? Who's stupid? Is Matt stupid?"

"No!"

"Go on! I want to hear you say it in a loud voice: *I am not stupid!*"

"Matt is not stupid," he says, with a laugh.

"And don't you forget it or I shall put caterpillars in your salad and give you a boil on the end of your nose!"

Suddenly, the laughter stops and he looks serious again.

"*Je voudrais te câliner.* I want to give you a hug, *Grand-mère Kate*."

My insides loop the loop.

"That could be a little difficult. I have a feeling you might travel through me and come out the other side if you tried to hug me! I would love to hug you too, Matt. Why don't you give your mum a hug – and make it a big one so that it's from me as well."

Shutters seem to descend and suddenly Matt's eyes and face are expressionless. I wonder how I've managed to put my foot in it this time?

"What's wrong? What's difficult about giving your mother a hug?"

"She didn't want to hug me. I heard her say that to François."

Appalled, I tell him he must have got it wrong.

"What did she say Matt? Do you remember her exact words?"

"She said that she wasn't ready to have a child and that it was all his fault."

"But just because you came along as a bit of a surprise doesn't mean that she doesn't love you now she has you. In fact, I *know* she loves you. You know how I can read your mind? Well, I can read hers too. She thinks about you nearly all the time and she wouldn't do that if she didn't care about you a lot."

Matt looks doubtful. To him, it's only logical to conclude that if you were not wanted then, why should you be loved now? Even worse, in his mind Matt believes he is unlovable and that his birth is somehow his fault. I can't bear to continue the conversation. How could he possibly think that Celia doesn't love him? No wonder he withdraws like a snail into its shell. I hastily change the subject without, as Thomas would say, stopping to think first. It's odd, I was never considered particularly spontaneous when I was alive. At least I don't think I was.

"Matt, would you like to go to Ireland and see the house in your picture and your grandfather?"

"And the parrot?"

"And the parrot."

"Yes, I would like that very much."

"Well, tell your mother that. Wait a little while though. I think she's had a bit of a shock over the picture. Give her time to get used to the idea of your dreaming it all in such incredible detail."

"D'accord!" Matt grins at me, "That means OK, *Grand-mère Kate!"*

"Oh, right! *D'accord*, Matt!"

Over the next few days, I watch as Celia gives flute lessons to a succession of not very eager or gifted pupils. She goes up to the small school to teach them. Occasionally, she goes to their houses. In the evenings, she sometimes looks after other people's children. It's hardly the ideal situation for Matt who, if there's no free bed available, curls up and goes to sleep on a couch or chair. I can see how short of money they are and how difficult life is for her. I hate to see her sitting alone at the table in the sparsely furnished kitchen after Matt's gone to bed. Each evening, she opens a small purse and counts the notes and coins into small heaps with a worried expression.

Yesterday, she encountered the man called François in the market. Matt was with her. Of course I couldn't understand what passed between the two adults but I could see how indifferent the man was to the boy. I also noticed how, in the other's presence, Matt became even more gawky and withdrawn. He refused to talk and turned away, slouching over to another stall where he stared at the courgettes and aubergines with unseeing eyes. In his mind, there was not just anger but also a good measure of misery. Silently, he accompanied Celia home when she'd finished her shopping. She soon gave up trying to get some response out of him. She was just too weary.

It's only today that Matt first broaches the subject of going to Ireland. He's picked his moment well. It's Sunday and Celia and he are sitting in the garden with glasses of lemonade she made the previous evening. They've eaten their midday meal and the early afternoon sun is pleasantly warm. I'm reclining in the arms of the large mimosa, looking down on them. They are both barefoot and dressed casually, not having been to church. I wonder what William would have said about their godlessness. A few years ago, he would have been shocked, but now . . .?

Matt snatches a quick look in my direction and telepaths a question.

"Shall I ask her now?"

"I think now is as good a time as any. Go on then!"

He takes a deep breath. "Mama?"

Celia raises her eyes from the book she's reading.

"Mm?"

"Can I ask you a question?"

Something in the way he says that makes my daughter lower the book.

"Well, what is it?"

"It's something very important . . ."

"Yes?"

I can't help feeling a little irritated with her. She's not making it very easy.

"Mama, you know how Matt dreamed about the house . . . and. . ." he's picking his words with care, "then Matt painted the picture?"

Celia seems suddenly to be very still. Her eyes watch his face without moving.

"Mm."

The words come out in a rush, all caution forgotten. "I want to go and see the house. I want to go and see *grand-père* and the parrot. Will you take me, please?"

Celia stares at him for a few minutes before answering.

"Why is it suddenly so important to go to Ireland? And why do you just want to see your grandfather and Minerva? What about your grandmother?"

"Oh, she's d- " I shoot out of the tree at such a rate I'm in danger of continuing down through the ground at Matt's feet. He gives me a startled look and stops speaking.

"She's what, Matt?"

"She's . . ." He casts around desperately for what his grandmother is – apart from dead.

"She's *with* grandfather?" I suggest hurriedly.

"She's with *grand-père*. So they will be together when we go and see them . . ."

Celia gives him a funny look.

"Why do I get the feeling there's something you're not telling me?"

Matt's assumed expression of innocent incomprehension doesn't seem to convince my daughter otherwise. She frowns slightly and then picks up her book again.

"I can't afford to take you to Ireland at the moment, Matt."

Matt gives me a look that says 'Can't you help? Can't you do something!'

"Leave it for the moment, Matt. Give your mother time to think about it."

"But . . ."

I find myself blurting out, "Would you like to come and watch me walk through a wall?"

He looks over at Celia who is apparently immersed in her book again. Then, trying unsuccessfully to hide a look of intense excitement, Matt slides off his chair and follows me around the end of the house. I have a quick look up and down the lane to make sure there's no one around to see Matt's possible reaction to his wall-commuting gran.

For maximum effect, I position myself at first-floor height; a good ten feet above my grandson's upturned face, which is now glowing with anticipation. Feeling a bit like a circus act, I ask him if he's ready.

"Yes, yes! Show me quickly before Mama wonders where I've gone."

I glide into position, a few feet from the white-washed wall and hold my arms out in front of me in good ghostly fashion. Slowly I propel myself forward until I feel the sun-warmed plaster against the ends of my fingers. Looking straight ahead, I move into and beyond the wall. At the other side, I turn and re-emerge to find Matt hopping from one foot to the other, grinning broadly.

"*Fantastique! Superbe! Merveilleux!*"

I rather gather that the demonstration is a success!

"What else can you do, *Grand-mère Kate?* Show me something else!"

He looks so happy! I run through some of the manoeuvres I have been practising in the last few weeks.

I cause a dozen or so small stones that are lying in the laneway to rise into the air and spin in a line, before letting them fall gently to earth. It looks rather good, even if I say so myself. Eat your heart out, ET! Then I place myself beside a young pine tree and think 'tree' as hard as I can. Gradually, I manage to assume the rough form of the tree so that there are two where once there was only one. This produces more exclamations of delight from Matt. It's difficult to maintain tree-shape for long but as I metamorphose back to my usual self, he begs me not to stop.

"*Encore!* Again!"

"Darling, I'm feeling a little tired."

"Please," he begs, "just one more trick!"

"All right but this has to be the last one for now."

I turn my attention to Matt's football, which is lying beside the broken gate. I raise it to the level of the top of the house and then make it float down in front of where he stands. He reaches out to touch it and the ball floats up again, above his head. Matt jumps and swats at it and the ball goes higher. Laughing, he picks up a stick and tries again to prod the swaying ball. It floats just out of reach, gyrating slowly.

"Matt! What are you doing?" Celia sounds thoroughly alarmed.

Too late, I let the ball bounce to the ground as Matt spins round to face his mother. She walks over and grabs his shoulder roughly.

"How did you do that with the ball?"

"What with the ball?"

Celia shakes him and then bends down and looks him straight in the face.

"Don't play games with me, Matt! I saw what you did with the ball just now. *How* did you make it do that?"

Before I can make any helpful suggestions to get him off the hook, Matt blurts out, "Magic!"

143

"What do you mean 'magic?'"

Matt's face goes blank.

"Magic," he repeats, in a sullen voice.

I see alarm and frustration written all over Celia's face. She's thinking, that on top of all the other problems she has with Matt, he now seems to be in league with sinister forces that enable him to move objects without touching them.

"I want you to come inside with me."

"I want to stay outside," he protests.

"Now! You'll come inside where I can keep an eye on you."

Still holding on to him, she marches him into the house while Matt sends out a barrage of furious messages to me.

"What can I do? Why can't I tell her about you? Why is she so angry?"

Thinking that perhaps it would be a good thing to keep out of the way, I tell him to try not to get upset and I will see him in a little while. Judging from Matt's expression, it's obvious he thinks that I'm chickening out. I tell myself that I'm trying not to complicate matters any further, but yes, I am chickening out. I just hope that Thomas didn't witness this last little fiasco of my making.

Chapter Fifteen

A letter has arrived for Celia from William! I recognise the handwriting immediately the postman gives her the envelope, leaning over the divided door, still astride his bike. He's young with a small moustache and I can tell he fancies my daughter from the way he stares at her. I don't like him and neither, thank goodness, does she.

"*Merci*," she says, with a brief smile and then turns away dismissively.

The wretched young man doesn't want to be dismissed and tries his best to engage her in conversation but my daughter has spotted the Irish stamp. She efficiently gives him the brush-off. I'm impressed! I was never able to do that. I didn't want to hurt people's feelings and was always an easy target for the village bore or any visiting Mormons. It drove William mad the way I seemed to be incapable of saying, 'No, thank you. We're not interested. Goodbye!'

She takes the letter over to the table and stares at it for a moment before sitting down and opening it. I move to behind her chair. I can't help myself but I just have to see what William's written. It's not a long letter:

Dear Celia,

Thank you for sending your address. I have wanted to contact you for some time but up until now it has not been possible.

I find it difficult to tell you this and I expect you will be very upset but you should know that your mother died six weeks ago. She had cancer and unfortunately the chemotherapy didn't help. I know how much she wanted to see you again and how sorry she was that things turned out the way they did.

I would like you to know that I also am sorry and, if it's not too difficult, I would be very pleased if you could manage to come home, even if it's only for a visit.

Your mother felt sure that one day you would come back but I realise that it won't be the same without her here to welcome you.

I hope that you don't feel it would be too uncomfortable for you. I can only repeat that you will be most welcome and I enclose a bank draft, which may come in useful, should you decide to make the journey.

Daddy.

I find this awkward letter strangely moving. How many drafts did it take for William to arrive at this one? It must have been so difficult for him to write and especially hard for him to say that he is sorry. The fact that he has, moves me most.

Celia folds the letter, puts it down on the table in front of her and bursts into tears. She buries her head in her hands and weeps so that tears drip onto the folded page.

It's awful to see her like this. I want to stroke her shorn head and hold her in my arms and tell her it's all right; that I remember what it was like when my own mother died. Although she and I were never very close, there was a sort of uneasy, unspoken love between us. When my father rang to tell me of her sudden death and used that ghastly phrase 'passed away' – as though she'd been casually handed on, like a parcel – I still remember how bereft I felt. Even up to the time of my own death, there were frequent occasions when I longed to know that she was there; even if it were only at the other end of a phone. Now it's my daughter's turn. Poor Celia!

She's just beginning to pull herself together when Matt comes into the room. He stops in his tracks when he sees his mother's swollen, red-rimmed eyes. I motion to him to go to her. Cautiously, he moves to the table and waits. It's obvious that he doesn't like to see her looking so upset but doesn't know what he should do.

"Mama?" he asks, nervously.

Celia quickly wipes her nose with the back of her hand, sniffs loudly and gives him a watery smile.

"Hi there!"

"What's the matter? Why are you crying?"

"I've had a letter from your grandfather and . . ."

"Does he want us to go and see him?"

"Yes, as a matter of fact, he does."

"Good! When are we going?"

"Matt, you don't understand. It's not as straightforward as you think. First of all, your grandfather doesn't know about you – yet –" Before Matt has a chance to respond, Celia hurries on. "And something awful has happened. Your grandmother has died." She looks at Matt anxiously.

"I know! Why didn't you tell *Grand-père* about Matt?" he asks, accusingly.

Celia stiffens and gives a small shiver, like an animal sensing something wrong with its environment.

"Hold on a moment! What do you mean, 'you *know*'?"

Too late, Matt realises that he's put his foot in it again, big-time. I can't think of any way out of this one and when the inevitable appealing glance comes, I just shake my head in despair. He turns his gaze on his mother instead.

"Matt's dream?" he suggests, hopefully.

We both look at Celia to see if she'll fall for it but she's looking confused and quite unconvinced by her son's dream theory.

Taking advantage of a gap in the conversation, Matt goes on the attack.

"Why didn't you tell *Grand-père* about Matt?"

Celia seems to be having difficulty coping with the conversation.

"What?"

"Why didn't you tell about Matt?" he repeats.

"Because . . . I don't know why, Matt. I'm starting to think I've been very foolish."

She looks as though she's about to cry again. All of a sudden, Matt walks over to his mother and puts his arms around her.

"Don't cry, Mama. It's all right."

This unexpected reversal of roles suddenly strikes Celia as bizarre and, rather shakily, she gives an uncertain laugh as she holds him to her.

"Thank you, Matt. I'm fine, really I am."

Without Matt noticing, I slip out into the garden. I don't want to be a distraction when it seems as though, possibly for the first time in my grandson's life, he's being given the chance to be the one who helps and is supportive.

I decide to hang out in the clouds for a bit. I'm rather thankful that Thomas doesn't seem to be around because I don't think he'd be too impressed with my performance over the past couple of days. I'm not deluding myself into thinking that he doesn't know exactly what's being going on but at least it's nice not to be reminded that I've handled things rather clumsily.

I climb to the right height from the point of view of temperature control; low enough to benefit from the warm sunlight and just high enough to catch a touch of cooling breeze. Matt would love it up here! It's the perfect place to play hide and seek among all these fat, rounded mounds of clouds.

I wander in and out of them, imagining castles and forests and lakes of blue sky; like a child who looks out of a plane window onto a fluffy, make-believe landscape outside. I'm enjoying myself enormously and it's a relief to leave the world and its problems behind for a short while. All at once, I become aware of a funny buzzing sound and then, before I can take evasive action, a small aircraft suddenly materialises out of a particularly solid-looking cluster of meringues and dollops of vanilla ice-cream, and motors past, nearly making me go into free-fall with fright. I rock a bit in the turbulence as it disappears as quickly as it came. I wonder what it would be like to be in the path of a jump jet. Disturbing, I should imagine!

I watch a pair of kestrels gracefully spiralling and hovering. I really ought to study them more closely. I'm sure I could learn a lot about riding the thermals. They've spotted me but they're not the slightest bit interested and keep their distance. I would hardly make an appetising snack and they know perfectly well that I'm no threat to them.

It's funny the sort of things you find yourself puzzling about when you're floating around up here: I was just thinking about how dirty one's car windscreen gets on long journeys. How do birds stop flies and other foreign bodies from getting in their eyes when they're travelling? You don't see many wearing goggles and if they *do* get something lodged in the corner of their eye, how do they get it out? Perhaps, if you listened carefully, you'd hear one saying to another, 'Don't worry, mate. Keep blinking and you'll be fine.'

One important thing I've learned up here is, never travel directly *under* a flock of birds. I swear they do it on purpose!

Celia's gone to see François, leaving Matt on his own in the house. She knew better than to ask him to go with her and from what I could make out from her thoughts, she didn't want him to accompany her. I get the feeling that she intends sorting out her relationship with the Frenchman once and for all. It's as if she wants to be completely sure that there is no future for them. I wish she would spare herself the anguish of confronting the man. I only saw him once and it was patently obvious that, as well as not wanting to have anything to do with his son, neither was he the slightest bit interested in Celia.

Matt has wandered out into the garden and is looking for

me. He's very good at this telepathy thing. He'd make an excellent spirit – he's a natural! As I come to earth, he gives me a worried look.

"Mama has gone to see *him*."

"The man who is your father?"

Matt's eyes fill with sudden tears.

"Matt doesn't want her to go to him. Matt wants to go to Ireland."

He is plainly frightened that François will say something that might make Celia feel she should stay on the island.

"Don't worry! I'm sure you'll go to Ireland with your mother but she has to tell François first, doesn't she?"

My grandson looks a little less anxious. I only hope I'm not storing up trouble by anticipating my daughter's next move. She's not stupid. She must know that the man isn't worth hanging around here for and Matt deserves to be in a place where he can have help. I nervously wonder what William's reaction will be when he is presented with a seven-year-old grandchild? We'll just have to cross *that* bridge when we come to it.

"*Grand-mère Kate?*"

"Yes, Matt?"

"Will you do more magic for me?" On seeing my look of indecision, he urges, "Please? Mama won't be back for ages."

"Well, all right but we must be careful this time. What would you like me to do?"

"Something new!"

I haven't tried this one before on anything except inanimate objects so I have to think hard. It takes two or three goes and then, to my grandson's delight, he finds himself slowly rising from the ground. I swear that his grin stretches from one ear to the other! When I've lifted him a foot off the grass, I turn him and gently float him towards the mimosa. After a few circles of the trunk and a couple of circuits round the garden, I'm beginning to feel the strain. I lower him carefully back to where he started. It's as though he's been struck dumb but I only have to look at his face to see that he's sublimely happy.

Finally, he says, in a hushed voice, *"Merci, Grand-mère Kate. Merci beaucoup!"*

Despite pleas for more, I meander upwards so that I can scan the lane. I'm anxious about Celia's imminent return.

"There'll be plenty of time for more," I tell him. "We don't want to make your mother worried again, do we?"

He shakes his head, suddenly solemn.

Chapter Sixteen

More tears! This time though, they are tears of anger on Celia's part.

I'd left Matt playing happily with his football and gone to see where my daughter was. I'd started to get warning signals and I just knew that all was not well. Now she's walking along the road towards the lane and her mind is bursting. From what I can make out of the jumbled emotions sloshing around like dirty washing in a washing-machine, François has suddenly turned all paternal and is threatening to take her to court if she takes *his* son out of France. And I hoped that it was going to be plain sailing! What worries me most about the situation is young Matt.

I follow her as she turns into the lane. She isn't sure how much to tell him but she knows that Matt will be heartbroken when he hears what has happened. Celia hasn't discovered why he's developed this sudden passion to go to Ireland. Although she's inclined not to believe his story about seeing the house in a dream, she can't see how else he could have known what it looked like. Matt being aware of his grandmother's death bothers her more than anything else.

She's starting to wonder if her son is some sort of psychic oddity and Celia doesn't much like the idea. She was, and I suppose still is, a rather pragmatic girl – seeing things in black and white; life was always straightforward. A thing was either right or wrong and there was no time to waste on ambiguous shades of pale grey.

She reaches the small gate that hangs crookedly from its hinges and as she walks towards the open door, Celia tells herself to stay calm for Matt's sake. She calls out to him.

"Where are you, Matt? I'm back!"

He comes running in from the garden. His bare feet and knees are dusty and his shorts torn. Matt scans her face for telltale signs that might help him guess what has happened in the meeting between his mother and 'that man' as he calls François in his mind.

I find it disturbing and yet, I suppose, understandable that the boy seems to really hate his father but then, children don't flourish on rejection. Celia's brave attempt at cheerfulness doesn't fool him for a moment. His face falls.

"What did he say?"

"François? Not very much really. We only talked for a little while."

I notice that neither of them refers to the man as father or papa. Matt looks impatient.

"But what did he *say*? Did you tell him we go to Ireland?"

"Matt, I never said that we would definitely go."

His look speaks volumes. Celia finds his stare disconcerting and makes a placatory gesture with her hands but Matt starts walking out of the room before she can say anything more.

At the door into the garden, he turns and says in a quietly determined voice, "Matt is going to Ireland and Mama wants to go too."

Celia is left staring after him.

It's late in the afternoon and Matt has wandered down to the cove at the far end of the lane. The air is full of the tang of wet seaweed. He seems very small and vulnerable as he perches on a rock, skinny legs startlingly pale against its rough, barnacled darkness. Matt stares morosely out to sea. Every now and then he hurls a stone into the greeny-blue water that surges around the rock.

He's refused to speak to me ever since his mother returned and I feel terrible. Although he is an adept student of telepathic communication, he can't block me out of his thoughts and I know he feels I've let him down badly. After a lot of patient prodding, I finally get him to respond.

"Matt, don't be angry! Just because everything isn't the way you would like it to be right now doesn't mean that it won't work out in the end, you know."

"You said we would go to Ireland."

Another stone is hurled into the water with a small plop.

"I know I did. I think that you'll still go but you have to be a little patient. You must understand that I haven't had all that much practice at being dead and I'm learning all the time but I promise that I will do my best to sort this out – just as soon as I can."

155

There is a hesitation before he replies.

"*D'accord.* OK."

His voice still sounds flat.

"You might have to help me. Do you think you could?"

The offhandedness vanishes and for the first time this afternoon, he looks enthusiastic.

"Matt would like that!"

I wonder in passing why he always refers to himself in the third person. Isn't that one of the symptoms of autism? Thomas told me not to put labels on the child and, even if I knew, would it make any difference? I'm hardly in the best position to read it up in textbooks in the library. I'm not sure in what way Matt can help remedy the situation concerning his father's newfound paternalism. I'm not even sure what I can do. I shall have to have a good think. I'm discovering that one of the troubles with seven-year-old boys is that everything has to be done instantly.

"Well, give me a little time to think over the problem and I'll tell you when I've decided what's the best thing to do. In the meantime, you be nice to your poor mum. It's not pleasant for her to have to go and argue with François. She will feel a lot better about things if you look after her. She needs you to be kind, Matt."

Perhaps it's asking a bit much of him but he nods gravely and looks much happier than he did when we first started the conversation. I leave him to make his own way back to the house and I ascend for a brainstorming session.

A day later – and I think that I have come up with quite a good idea. As soon as Matt comes back from school, I perform semaphore behind Celia's back to attract his attention and get him to go into the garden. Attempting to hide a grin, he quickly finishes his plate of rice and mince and gets down from the table. I intervene before he can go any further.

"What about carrying your plate and glass to the sink?"

"Matt forgot," he unthinkingly says out loud.

Celia regards him with the slightly apprehensive look that she's started to give him recently.

"Forgot what, Matt?"

He goes pink and involuntarily glances over in my direction. Celia swings around in her chair and also looks over to the general area where I'm cringing on my grandson's behalf.

"What is it? What did you see?"

"Nothing," he blurts out. "Matt sees nothing. Matt is going in the garden."

"Just a moment!" Celia's voice is sharp. "Why did you say just now that you forgot?"

I know I shouldn't encourage him to tell fibs but this is all becoming more than I can stand. I may be invisible but I tell you, my blood pressure is getting raised to the point where something is going to have to give.

"Tell her you forgot to fetch your ball from the lane, anything! But tell her something quickly!" I urge him.

"Matt's ball is in the lane."

"Is that what you forgot?"

"Yes," says Matt, all wide-eyed innocence.

"You'd better go and fetch it then," replies Celia, still looking suspicious.

Once outside, he rushes round to the end of the house with me in hot pursuit.

"Matt, you must be more careful!"

"Sorry, *Grand-mère Kate*. Matt forgot," he says automatically as he scoops up the battered football.

"And don't you 'Matt forgot' me, my lad." He gives me an enchanting smile and I melt. "It' s too difficult trying to talk during the daytime when your mother's around. I shall come and see you when you're tucked up in bed tonight. All right?"

"Right," he answers brightly. "when Matt . . . when *I* am in bed."

"Yes, when *you* are in bed!" I say, with a smile. There! He can do it! Perhaps I've been worrying too much about things like that. "Well done, Matt. That's splendid!"

I can't help feeling chuffed. Perhaps I can really help him so that he will find life easier. I hope so.

I watch him as he disappears around the corner of the house, clutching the ball to his chest. It's only then that I see Celia's tense face looking out of an upstairs window. She's staring down at the place her son had been standing in a moment ago, apparently talking to thin air. Oh, not again! It's as though every time I try and do something to help Matt, I just end up making life more difficult for him. Perhaps he'd be better off without a granny like me.

My daughter's gone to bed early. She looks exhausted. She can think of nothing but problems: the problem of getting back to Ireland, which she now wants to do, the problem of dealing with François and of trying to understand his puzzling Gallic twists and turns. Above all, her mind is full of the problem of her son's recent strange and disturbing behaviour. Why has he started holding intense conversations with imaginary beings? After tossing and turning for an hour, she finally falls asleep.

For a little while, I stand at the bottom of her bed and watch her as she sleeps. There are the beginnings of frown-lines lightly pencilled on her smooth forehead and her face has the bruised look of someone who's nearly too tired to sleep. An almost imperceptible breeze nudges the muslin curtain that is hooked crookedly over the shuttered window. Looking round the room with its basic furnishing of bed, chair and wardrobe, I realise that my daughter's rather Bohemian life style upsets me. I suppose it's because I never had to do without. Whatever the regrets and little miseries were that I experienced, I was always surrounded by comfort and for some crazy reason, I imagined that Celia would always be comfortable too.

An owl hoots once outside, making her stir and mutter something in her sleep. Her eyelids quiver. She's dreaming of the house in the red glen.

Eschewing the wall route, I take the long way round to where Matt also has fallen asleep. He lies, half-covered by a light blanket, spread-eagled in his bed. His T-shirt is rucked up above his waist so that he looks a bit like an undernourished plucked chicken. Getting him to waken is like trying to raise the dead. Actually, being dead myself, I don't think I would be at all difficult to raise. I seem to take catnaps on the wing and I'm extremely easily disturbed!

Matt's dreams are full of jets and submarines and fast cars. I eventually manage to get him to wake up by forcing myself in-between all the machinery whizzing around in his head until there is nothing but my face left in his dream.

"Wake up, Matt! We have some planning to do."

Instantly, he is sitting up, wide-awake. He looks all tousled and I wish I was substantial enough to hold him on my lap and cuddle him while I explain what should be done to make it possible for him to go to Ireland. Being a seven-year-old male means that he would most likely hate the idea of a cuddle. Just an occasional brief hug perhaps!

"*Bon soir, Grand-mère Kate*. What are we going to do?"

"It'll have to be up to you, Matt. Now listen carefully. If you can get your mother to pretend that she *has* to go to Ireland because of your poor old granny falling off her perch . . ." Matt giggles, "and if François won't allow her to take you with her, then she will sadly have to go without you. She will just have to leave you behind with him. Do you think that he will have the time" (I'm careful not to add, or the inclination) "to look after a small boy when he comes home tired after a day's work?"

Matt's eyes gleam in the nearly dark room.

"*Non, vraiment non!*" he replies in an excited whisper. "He would not like that!"

"So, do you think you could persuade your mother to say that to him?"

"Yes! *I* will do that tomorrow!"

"Good boy! Now, go back to sleep and sweet dreams!"

Almost before I'm out of the room, Matt is dreaming again. He is sitting at the controls of some shiny red vehicle with tyres the width of a tractor's and an engine that growls like an angry panther.

It's seven o'clock in the morning and already the day is luminously bright and warm. Celia is watching in astonishment

160

as Matt slowly and deliberately ties each shoelace. She shakes her head.

"When did you learn to do that? A week ago, there would have been a mighty battle to get you to tie up just one shoe."

I can see that Matt is being extra-specially careful not to answer any questions without first thinking through his response.

"I have been practising. *C'est une surprise pour toi!*"

"Well, it's a lovely surprise. Come on! Come and have some *pain au chocolat* which is *my* surprise for you."

When they've both sat down for their breakfast, Matt takes a big gulp of hot milk from his bowl and then nibbles at the end of a fresh roll which oozes dark chocolate onto his fingers. It smells delicious and in spite of no longer possessing any internal organs, I nearly feel hungry. He watches his mother for a moment before speaking.

"Mama, I have a great plan."

Celia looks amused.

"What is it, this great plan?"

He takes a deep breath and wades in.

"If you tell François that you have to go to Ireland because of the death of *Grand-mère Kate*, he will not be happy. If you tell him that you will have to leave Matt behind and *he* will have to look after him – then he will be even more not happy. *N'est-ce pas?*" Matt beams at her. "So, all you have to do is that. It is easy!"

Celia gives him the uncomfortable look and is silent for a moment. She's wracking her brains, trying to remember if she ever told Matt that his grandmother's name was Kate. She supposes she must have. My daughter considers the 'great plan', then she too smiles.

"You know, Matt. It might just work, you clever thing!"

Celia leans over and gives his chocolate-covered hand a squeeze.

Matt is sending out smug messages over the airwaves.

"See, *Grand-mère Kate!* I said Matt would do it and I did!"

Chapter Seventeen

As soon as Matt went off to school, Celia set out for the eel-sheds where François works. She looked so pretty and rested after her long night's sleep. She was wearing the blue cotton dress I saw her in when I first came to the island and a light green and blue Indian shawl over her shoulders. I wonder what William will make of the little silver nose-stud and the half-moon of multiple silver earrings that adorn each ear?

I didn't go along, partly because I'd rather not, in case things go wrong and partly because I wouldn't understand much of what was being said. So I'm waiting here, twiddling my thumbs and crossing my fingers – if that's possible. It is! I've just tried it.

I can't help feeling proud of my daughter! She seems to speak the language so fluently and just as fast as the locals do. No wonder Matt can switch backwards and forwards from one to the other. I wonder how long it will take for his French accent to fade when he's back in Ireland. It sounds delightful to me but I wouldn't want him to appear too different when he gets there after what's happened here with the boys at school.

That's something that puzzles me. Young children never judge others. At what age do they suddenly decide that being different is wrong and something to be feared and even attacked?

She's been gone for a long time. It only takes twenty minutes to walk to the factory and Celia's been away for nearly an hour. Still, it's given me the chance to do a quick check on Matt and he's fine. Didier and Claude haven't accepted him but at least now they give him a wide berth. Because of this, the hangers-on in the baiting game have also stopped making Matt's life a misery. *Le Prof* – as the children call him – is a disgrace though! He *must* know that my grandson has some sort of a learning problem and yet he makes no effort whatsoever to help him. He didn't do anything about the bullying either. When Matt stumbles over a simple reading exercise, the man just snorts and makes a remark that turns the poor boy bright red. Then Matt becomes even more confused and starts dropping things.

It was getting a bit crowded up here on the roof a little while ago. I was suddenly joined by an elderly couple who apparently used to own the house. They had come back to the island to visit one of their sons. From what they said, it sounded as though the lad had been rather wild and they were extremely worried. They said their Guardian Angel (from Senegal) had been very helpful in locating him and now that their minds were at rest, they just wanted to visit the home they'd lived in for all their married life before they went back up. The wife didn't speak English but the old man and I were able to make ourselves understood through a mixture of sign language and a hilarious hotch-potch of words that we knew in each other's respective languages.

They were very sweet people – although I had to try and stay upwind because his spirit still had a powerful odour of garlic clinging to it. When I told him about the trouble my daughter was having with François, he shook his head gravely and said, 'I know 'im. *Il n'est pas gentil, ce jeune homme. Attention, eh, Madame!*'

They both seemed relaxed and happy about going back up and quite prepared to accept whatever it was that would happen next. I would very much have liked to arrange a rendezvous. In the end, I decided I'd better not as I don't know when or where I'm going next.

The last view I had of them was as they slowly floated up to the sky, side by side. Just before they dissolved into the clouds, they seemed to glow with a strange luminescence and then they were gone.

At last! I see Celia's blue dress in the distance. I can't wait a moment longer to see if she's been successful or not. I propel myself at high speed along the lane towards her so that I can see her face.

She resembles a cat that's just demolished an exceedingly large bowl of cream! She also looks ten years younger and is walking with a bounce in her step that's been missing during my time on the island. She's thinking of how she will tell Matt the good news when he comes home for the midday meal and is anticipating the look of pleasure on his face when he hears that, after all, they are going to Ireland.

As she nears the house, her step slows. The fact that they will be going back to the house in the glen and that I will not be there to greet them floods back into her mind. She suddenly looks stricken.

"Oh, Mum! I'm so sorry!" she whispers out loud.

Words like 'foolish' and 'selfish' and 'too late' are swimming around in her mind. Again, I wish I could tell her that it really doesn't matter and that I love her dearly but she's right; it *is* too late to go into all of that now. She'll just have to make the best of it and it's tough. I know that.

Matt comes pelting into the house as Celia is laying things out on the table for their midday meal. She looks up with a smile as he stands, panting, in the doorway. My grandson doesn't waste his words.

"We are going?"

"Yes, Matt, we are going," my daughter says, laughing.

Matt hurls himself across the kitchen and for the first time, I see him spontaneously embrace his mother, holding on to her tightly for a few seconds. His eyes are squeezed shut and his face is radiant. Then he breaks away self-consciously. Taking a step back from her, he attempts to regain his composure.

"That is good," he says, in a nonchalant voice.

As they eat, Matt bombards Celia with questions.

"Did you say to him the things I tell you to say?"

"I did."

"Did François look funny when you said that he would have to take care of Matt?"

Celia gives a chuckle.

"Very funny."

"*How* did he look, Mama?"

"Well, you know how old Monsieur Charpentier looks when he thinks he has managed to cheat you out of your change and you hold out your hand while you wait for the rest?"

"Yes! Sort of like one of his dead fish with its mouth wide open!"

"Exactly! Well, that's a bit like the expression on François' face – only his eyes were on stalks as well!"

Matt hugs himself in delight. Then a new barrage of questions start.

"When are we going?"

"As soon as I can get it arranged. At the end of next week, I expect. I have to ring your grandfather and see if it fits in with his plans."

A horrible thought dawns on Matt. He looks at Celia anxiously.

"*Pour voyager, il faut un passeport!* Do I have a passport?"

"You are on my passport, so it's all right. Don't worry!"

Matt wants to know how many rooms there are in the house in Ireland. In which one will he sleep? Will he be able to teach Minerva to speak French? Can he climb the mountain opposite the house? He seems unstoppable! Finally, Celia holds up a hand to shut him up.

"That's enough! I have a lot of things to do. I know you want to find out all about Ireland but you will have to be rationed. Five questions only each day from now on!"

Matt looks appalled.

"Only five?"

167

"Five," repeats Celia firmly as she gets up from the table.

I must say, I'm enjoying these last few days before *'le grand voyage'* as Matt insists on calling it. Although there are moments when Celia is racked with guilt over my death, they both seem to have taken on a new lease of life. Matt's buttoning and shoelace-tying skills are coming on well and he's almost completely stopped using the third person when he's talking about himself. I'm afraid I haven't been much use to him with his reading though. I'm pretty sure that he's going to need expert help in that particular area.

With great difficulty, he's managed to stick to asking his mother five questions a day but of course he's been cheating. When he's used up his daily quota, he asks me at least another twenty!

Celia is dashing around, trying her best to conjure money out of her pupils for their flute lessons, cleaning the house, paying her bills and packing up. It's good that William's bank draft was more than enough to cover the cost of travelling. I'm pretty sure that she wouldn't have been able to settle all her debts without it. As for the packing – they have so few belongings that I think everything will fit into two medium-sized suitcases.

Matt can hardly sleep with the excitement of it all. He's just found out, that after travelling on the small ferry to the mainland, they are to take the TGV to Paris, then a coach to the airport where they will fly direct to Dublin. William is to meet them at Dublin airport and drive them to the house.

"*Grand-mère Kate*! I can't wait for two more whole days," he complained mournfully after Celia had kissed him goodnight and gone downstairs. He wasn't too impressed with my reply.

"There's nothing you can do about it, Matt. You'll just have to!"

"I could fly with you. You know, like I did in the garden only more high and more fast. *Pourquoi pas?*"

I just looked at him and then he grinned and gave a very Gallic shrug.

"OK! Not a good idea!"

"No," I agreed. "How would you explain *that* to your mother?"

"With difficulty?" said Matt, his laughter echoing in my head.

Now we are sitting together in the garden under the old mimosa. Its feathery leaves make flecks of sunlight move backwards and forwards like shoals of tiny minnows across my grandson's shoulders and dark hair.

We had a spectacular thunderstorm and heavy rain last night and all the plants and trees are giving off an invigorating perfume that makes me feel pleasantly dizzy. As for the flowers! Remember what I said about, now I'm dead, my being able to hear them hum? Well, this morning, they'd give the Berlin Philharmonic a run for its money.

Actually, the storm took me by surprise. I'd been helping Matt with a numbers game when it suddenly struck. I know I could have bypassed it and waited high up, well above the thunderclouds, until it was all over. It was an extraordinary sensation when I went outside, to feel the raindrops streaming through me. The electricity in the air made me tingle all over like an over-active lightning conductor. All in all, it was an exhilarating experience!

Matt liked it too. Although, I do feel that he's getting so used to the idea of his dead granny being around that he's becoming just a little blasé. At the height of the storm, he suggested that it would be a good idea to run a test to see how a direct lightning strike might affect my system. When I declined to position myself on top of the church tower with my arms raised, he was quite downcast for a while.

Celia has gone down to the quayside to buy some fish for their supper, which gives us a chance for yet more questions.

"Tell me, *Grand-mère Kate*. Is it always raining in Ireland?"

"No, not at all. It rains more than here though."

"Claude says that Ireland is covered in bogs and mud and water because it always rains."

"I think young Claude is just a little bit jealous that he isn't getting the chance of going, don't you?"

"It's possible. But *Le Prof* says that Ireland it is called the 'Emerald Isle' because it is green and it is green because it rains."

"Yes, it rains some of the time but not all the time. Believe me!"

"Does *Grand-père* have a dog?"

"Only Minerva. She's quite enough of a handful."

"Will she like me?"

"I think she will like you very much. Especially if you feed her little pieces of fruit. She adores plums for some reason but don't give her too much or it will upset her insides," I warn, remembering the time the parrot nearly died. "Minerva escaped from her cage one day when I was out and your grandfather was working in his study. She found the fruit bowl and spent a happy morning attacking all the bananas, apples and pears she could get her beak into. She also found a bag on the kitchen table with a pound of plums inside. That evening she became very ill and she couldn't stop . . ."

"Shitting?" interjects Matt with enthusiasm.

Except the way he pronounces it sounds more like sheeting.

"Exactly! Anyway, she was too weak to sit on her perch any more and she was huddled up on the floor of her cage, looking dreadful. So do you know how I cured her?"

"How?"

"I poured a lot of good cognac into an eggcup and took her out of her cage, opened her beak and poured the lot in!"

"Mon Dieu!" exclaims my grandson. "And suddenly she was better?"

"I put her back in her cage and because it was very late, I went to bed. When I got up next morning, the first thing I did was go and see Minerva. She was sitting up on her perch, happy as anything and talking hard."

I seem to remember that the reason I was quite sure she was well on the way to recovery that morning was that Minerva was swearing like a trooper as she greeted me with her little welcome dance.

"I will be most careful," Matt assures me.

Then he asks a question that I'd rather been hoping he wouldn't.

"Grand-mère Kate? Why did not my mother tell Grand-père and you when I was born?"

"Haven't you asked your mother?" I say, playing for time.

171

"I asked her the other day and she said because she was stupid." He is concentrating hard on trying to find out what I am thinking, so I have to be careful here. Matt continues, "I do not think that is a good reason. Mama is not stupid," he says, with deadly logic.

"I agree, Matt. However, when you were born, your mother was only nineteen, which is very young to have a baby. I think that François left her to look after you all on her own. I don't know how much she's told you about why she left home. I don't think your mama was stupid but I think she was very young, very confused and probably quite frightened. Unfortunately for her and for me, she was also too proud to ask us for help and we didn't know how to find out where she was. Can you understand a little bit what it must have been like for her?"

"A little bit, I think." Matt tries hard to take it all in. It is a new concept for him that a parent can feel vulnerable and frightened – just like a child. "I think it is sad that it was like that for her. I did not know," he adds, almost guiltily.

"There was no reason for you to know. If she found it difficult to talk about, how could you know?"

"I do know that François has a wife."

I am shocked.

"You mean that François was already married when you were born?"

"*Non*. He got married *il y a deux ans* . . . two years ago."

Now I'm the one feeling guilty. It's just that the idea of Celia having a child by a married man would have seemed doubly sad. I briefly think back to a certain time in my own married life.

I must have dropped my guard because Matt suddenly asks, "Who is Milo?"

It's just as well that ghosts can't blush. Confining my thoughts into the 'to be read' area and the 'definitely out of bounds' area, I give Matt a bright smile.

"Just a very dear friend whom I haven't seen for a long, long time."

I am thankful to see that Celia's just coming in the gate, carrying a plastic bag of fish in one hand and a large bunch of herbs in the other.

"Go and greet your mother. I will see you later."

"OK! *Grand-mère Kate*," he says, cheerfully.

Today is the day of *le grand voyage* and I am going on ahead to see what is happening at William's end. I have explained that to Matt, who seemed sad that I wasn't going to keep them company on the journey. I consoled him with the idea that there would be so much for him to see and hear and smell that he wouldn't have the time or the opportunity for conversations with a dead gran.

"A gran who has fallen off her perch, just like Minerva!" he said, with wicked glee.

Even though it will only be for a short while, I'm going to miss them. It will be awful when Thomas finally tells me that my time's up in Limbo. I feel that I'm only just getting to know the pair of them. I suppose it has to happen sooner or later but it will be like dying a second time. Even worse – because I will be leaving behind a daughter whom I have grown to love all over again and an adorable grandson who I never knew existed until now.

Chapter Eighteen

I've never seen William like this before. Celia and Matt arrive tonight and he's in a complete tizzy, rushing around the place like a mad thing. He's had Mrs Byrne up from the village for the last couple of days to spring-clean the house from top to bottom and even Minerva's cage has had a scrub down and she's been given a splendid new water-holder.

My old parrot was so disgusted by all the upheaval, she really went over the top with her swearing. If I hadn't stepped in and told her I'd strangle her if she didn't shut up, I think Mrs Byrne might have been stopped in her tracks. As it was, the woman was so intrigued at 'getting inside the Fitzgeralds',' her curiosity blunted her sensibilities and she courageously managed to ignore the expletives issuing from the cage in the pristine kitchen.

I think it's quite probable that no one from the village has been in the house since I was taken ill in March. Up until then, only a handful of people called or were invited by me. William has an aversion to visitors. He always said it made it impossible for him to concentrate on his writing and he felt as though the house was being invaded. I thought his attitude was a bit extreme. It's not as though any of my friends behaved like rampaging Goths or Vandals.

I wasn't present when Celia made the phone call to William, asking him if she could come home. She must have found it difficult to tell him that he has a seven-year-old grandson. I wonder what his reaction was! The fact that he's obviously said that they can come is a good sign.

He's still sleeping in the small bedroom off his study, which means that Celia will probably be in the main bedroom and Matt will have the spare room just along the corridor from her.

It must have been a frightful scramble to get everything ready in time. Even the grass has been cut but it's obvious that William hasn't managed to get anyone up to the house to do any real gardening. As I wander around outside, I can't help feeling rather melancholy. I worked really hard out here for years and years and in just six months, nature seems to be intent on getting her own back.

I miss the dogs too. Sam and his lovable offspring, Samson. I know that he sired several litters of pups over the years. If I'd stayed hale and hearty, perhaps when he'd died I could have had a puppy called Samsgranson – very Viking!

October has just begun and the contrast between the island and the red glen couldn't be more marked. There, the sun still shines strongly and Matt could play outside most days in just a T-shirt and shorts. Here, there is a chill dampness to the evening air that makes me want to go inside to the warm kitchen where the ancient stove pumps out the heat. This morning, the newly cut grass was dusted with frost and the surface of the birdbath was laced with a cobweb of ice. It's a good thing that the windows are all double-glazed or the pair of them would be frozen.

The larches have turned a marvellous golden toffee colour and the ground is littered with a confetti of fallen red and yellow leaves from the birches. I often used to wonder if the glen's Irish name, *Gleannruadh*, meant the glen of the fox or whether it referred to the reddish colour of the branches of some of the willows (known locally as sallies) in wintertime. Or perhaps whoever named it was thinking of the clusters of scarlet berries that adorn the glossy hollies lining the valley's gently climbing road. Whatever the reason, the name suits it well.

Six o'clock and William is having a cup of coffee before he sets off for the two-hour journey to Dublin airport. It's just over two weeks since I was last here and the change I noticed in him that evening when Veronica told him she loved him, is even more marked. His features seem somehow gentler and more sad – although I think he will never look benign.

The way he talked to gossipy Mrs Byrne surprised me. She would have been just the sort of woman in the past to make him run for cover. In the kitchen this afternoon, he was patient and courteous in his dealings with her. I think she was surprised too. I could hear her thoughts as she busily revised her opinions of 'that Mr FitzGerald'. I get the feeling that something or someone has made the William I knew less arrogant. Mrs Byrne thinks it's 'because of the death of that poor wife of his'. She'd have a seizure if she knew that 'the poor wife' was relaxing on the kitchen sofa while Mrs Byrne stirred three heaped spoonfuls of sugar into her cup of stewed tea.

William's feeling nervous. Why shouldn't he? He hasn't seen Celia for over eight years and before she left home she let him know quite clearly what she thought of him – none of it complimentary. A girl of eighteen does an awful lot of growing up by the time she reaches twenty-six; especially when she's become a mother.

And there's Matt. How will William relate to him? The boy appears far more French than Irish in his accented speech and mannerisms. Will William look at Matt's dark eyes and hair and be struck by the physical similarity to himself at the same age?

As he sits there with his coffee, William is also wondering how different this impending reunion with his errant daughter would have been had I not died. I don't flatter myself that he's missing me desperately. I just get the feeling that he thinks it would be a lot easier to have me around, in spite of his relationship with Veronica.

Her existence is bothering him too. He's hoping that, having told her he doesn't want her here for a couple of days, she'll not stage an untimely entrance and make an already tricky situation yet more difficult.

With a sigh, he rises from the table and takes his cup and saucer over to the draining board. William casts a glance at Minerva. He's noticed that she's been unusually silent for the last while. That's because I'm standing beside her, looking threatening, and she's on her best behaviour. She keeps giving me sideways stares with one wicked little eye. William comes over and checks her water and food levels and then stands by the cage for a moment, puzzled.

"You feeling all right, Minerva?" he enquires.

I'm glad he's got round to talking to her. He never did

177

that before. Minerva observes him coldly and then slowly and deliberately rotates herself on her perch so that her scarlet tail feathers are pointing in his direction. She's thinking roughly along the lines of: 'Maybe I'm not allowed to swear but I don't have to look at the silly sod.' William shakes his head, hoping that the bird isn't sickening for something. He picks up his car keys from the table and goes towards the door. Minerva stays with her back to him until she hears it close. Then, giving me a quizzical look, she swivels round on her perch.

"Who rattled his cage?" she asks, sotto voce.

I've decided against accompanying William to Dublin. Goodness knows what it would be like for someone like myself, attempting to keep my equilibrium in a busy airport. There could be dozens of other spirits clogging up the air space and just think of all those people in planes taking off and landing! I was going to say that I'd be taking my life in my hands – but you know what I mean.

Also, I don't want to distract Matt when he's meeting his grandfather for the first time. So I'm staying put and keeping Minerva company. As stroking her with my hand is no longer an option, I've discovered that with my new telekinetic abilities, I can use a twig from the garden to scratch the back of her head. When I first introduced it into the cage, she nearly had a fit and thought I was about to poke her with it. Stupid bird! Now, she loves it. Her head tilts forwards as I gently tickle her neck feathers, her eyes close and she makes little crooning sounds of approval. I do hope she'll allow Matt to make friends with her.

They're finally here! They sit around the kitchen table and all three of them seem hopelessly tongue-tied. It's nearly midnight and both Celia and Matt are exhausted after their long journey. William's gone all formal – a habit he always had when he wasn't sure how to handle a situation. He's already asked Celia twice if she would like another cup of tea and whether Matt's hot milk was the right temperature.

Celia seems to be too overwhelmed at being home again to contribute much in the way of conversation. Finally, she shepherds a zombie-like Matt off to bed. Ten minutes later, she reappears.

"I think I'll go to bed too. Thank you for collecting us from the airport. I'd forgotten what a tiring journey it is. I'll see you in the morning."

William has been absent-mindedly stacking mugs into the dishwasher. He turns to look at her, trying not to let his eyes home in on the disconcerting silver ladybird decorating the side of his daughter's nose. I just *knew* that he'd have a problem with that! He sees it as another sign of the rebellious streak in Celia's character.

"Right! See you in the morning then. Goodnight."

At the same time as he says this, he's thinking, 'This is never going to work. She still doesn't like me. She can't even bring herself to call me by a name – not even "father".'

As Celia walks down the passage to where I used to sleep, she's thinking, 'Oh, God! Perhaps coming back wasn't such a wonderful idea after all. He's just going to spend his time staring at my pierced nose and short hair and he'll be so put off by them, he won't give me a chance.' She puts her head into Matt's room. He's fast asleep; a small hump under the blankets and old-fashioned eiderdown.

Quietly, she closes his door and makes her way to her room. When Celia left, William and I were still sleeping in the double bed in this room. It hasn't changed at all. Still the same pale green walls with the white ceiling and window frames. Still the same rather worn rose-pink carpet and curtains and the bedside lamp with the dent in the shade where I once dropped it. Still the same furniture.

Even though she's so tired, after closing the curtains my daughter stands for several minutes at the foot of the bed. Her eyes take in the room's details: the painting she did when she was fifteen of the view from the top of the valley, which I proudly had framed, the rosewood dressing-table with its delicate sycamore inlay that my parents gave me for my twenty-first birthday, a small Wedgwood vase, a crackle-glaze ceramic dove in white that I loved, a sandalwood trinket box. She runs her fingers lightly over its spice-scented carved top. All these things hold memories for her.

Slowly, she approaches the wardrobe in the corner, her reflection slightly distorted in its long mirror. Celia's remembering the afternoon so long ago when she and her schoolfriend Becky dressed up and a bottle of perfume was shaken until the last drop fell. She gives a little shiver then opens the wardrobe door. All my clothes are as I left them. She takes one look and then slams the door shut. Throwing herself onto the bed, she starts to cry. Hopeless, muffled sobs that won't be heard in another room.

I feel mixed emotions as I look at my daughter: sad that she is miserable yet knowing that she must grieve and that her tears are a healthy sign. After a while, she quietens and falls into a profound sleep. Floating it across the room, I cover her with the spare blanket that Mrs Byrne has left on the wooden chest at the end of the bed. Then I slip away, leaving her to a much-needed rest.

William is first up and, having collected the Saturday *Irish Times* from the village, is having some tea and toast alone in the kitchen. It's well after nine and he's wondering if he should take Celia a cup or leave her to sleep. A door creaks and opens a few inches to partly reveal a tousled Matt in his new blue pyjamas. Before he can spot me, I secrete myself high up in the least well-lit corner of the ceiling. I want to witness this first real exchange between grandfather and grandson without any input from me.

Matt hesitates on the other side of the door, unsure if he should go on or go back. Minerva cranes her neck to see what's happening at the other side of the room but the fridge blocks her view.

"You'd better come in or you'll let all the heat out of the kitchen," says William in an unintentionally gruff voice.

Matt slips into the room, obediently closing the door behind him. He approaches the tall, gaunt man at the table with caution. William waves his hand in the direction of the cereal bowls at the other end of the table.

"Help yourself. It's all there, ready for you."

Silently, Matt helps himself to cereal, pours milk into a mug and sits down opposite the window so that he can watch the fascinated parrot. She claws her way diagonally across the cage to get a better vantage point. For the moment, she's not talking either. It's agony up here. I wish

William and Matt would say something to each other but neither of them seems to know where to start.

Matt is munching on his sixth mouthful when Minerva decides to help things along. She gives an introductory croak and then launches into song.

"*What shall we do with the drunken sailor? What shall we do with the drunken sailor? What shall we . . .*"

Matt is transfixed, spoon halfway between bowl and mouth. He swallows and turns towards William.

"I did not know that parrots *sing*," he says, in an awed voice.

William lowers his paper.

"Your mother always said that Minerva has perfect pitch."

"What is perfect pitch?"

"I think it means when you always remember which note to start on and you always get the tune absolutely right." There's a pause and then he asks, "Do you . . . like to sing?"

"*Non,*" comes the succinct reply. "But, I like sometimes to paint."

"Watercolour or oils?"

"I have only painted with watercolour."

Apparently having exhausted that topic of conversation, William retreats behind his paper while Matt stolidly works his way through his bowl of cereal.

After a few minutes, Minerva casts a beady eye in my direction before giving her imitation of an owl. It's a very good imitation and Matt's impressed. He gulps down his milk and then carries his empty bowl and mug over to the sink.

"Can I go and talk to Minerva?"

"You can but watch out for her beak – it can be dangerous if she's not in a good mood."

"How do you know if she's in a good mood?"

William considers the question for a moment.

"I think if she's singing, that means you can probably take it for granted she's in a good mood."

I join Matt by the cage, making him jump slightly. After telepathing to him that it's really good to see him again, I suggest that he tickle the back of Minerva's head with the end of his finger. He sticks a tentative finger in through the bars and starts to gently stroke the back of the bird's head. Minerva is charmed! She bows her head and croons. William, who has been watching them over the top of his paper, looks surprised.

"She must like you. She never did that for anyone except . . ." he flounders, wondering if he should mention my name.

"Except for *Grand-mère Kate*?" asks Matt, stroking away.

"Who? . . . Oh, I see! Yes, except for your Grandmother Kate," says William, thankful that referring to me hasn't upset the boy.

Being with Minerva seems to relax my grandson and before the unsuspecting William knows what's happening, the floodgates open and the questions begin.

"*Grand-papa?* Why are some of Minerva's feathers missing?"

I can tell that although he doesn't show it, William rather likes being called 'Grand-papa'.

"I suspect it's got something to do with being in a cage and not in her natural habitat."

"What is habitat?"

"Where she was born. Where she belongs, back in West Africa."

"So, she is not happy?"

"She's happy enough. Minerva just gets a little bored every now and then and when she does, she pulls out a few feathers."

"Ouch! It must hurt her to do that."

Behind his paper, William gives one of his rare smiles.

"I would think it is quite likely to be a case of 'ouch!'"

I'm going to slip away. They seem to be getting along fine. Sadly, I'm not sure that William will find it as easy when it comes to talking to his daughter.

Lunchtime and things aren't going too well. An hour ago, William was outside with Matt, getting in some wood for the stove, when the telephone rang. Celia answered it.

"Hello?"

There was a brief pause at the other end and then a woman's voice replied.

"Hello! Is that Celia?"

"Yes," said my daughter, puzzled as to the identity of the other.

"It's Veronica! You remember! I was a great friend of your mother's."

"Oh, yes. I remember. How are you?"

"Fine! But I'm dying to see you and Matt. I wondered if you would mind if I dropped in around twelvish tomorrow?"

Before she had time to think about it properly, Celia found herself inviting Veronica to come and have Sunday lunch with them. After a few more exchanges, Veronica said she had to go and rang off with a 'can't wait to see you again'. Celia was left feeling that her mother's friend had been planning to drop in tomorrow, invitation or no invitation. Anyway, she wondered, how did Veronica know about her coming home and even more strange, who had told her about Matt? Veronica could only have got that sort of information from William. *My daughter, with her woman's intuition, feels that something is not quite right but she's not sure yet what it is.*

When Matt and William reappeared, arms full of logs, she watched her father carefully as she told him about Veronica's call and the impending visit planned for the next day. She could see how he immediately looked uneasy and when he said he would ring and put her off to another time, Celia insisted that he do no such thing.

"No, don't do that! I would like to see her again. It will be interesting after all this time," she said firmly.

Celia knew that William wasn't too happy about it. *Oh dear! And I thought, last time I was here, that Veronica seemed to have grown more sensible. I suppose it just goes to show that you can't expect people to change too rapidly and too completely.*

Now, there's a bit of an atmosphere around the table. Matt's aware of it but has successfully tuned it out and is studying Minerva's every move while he mechanically shovels his way through the meal. William is feeling resentful of the fact that his prodigal daughter has made him feel guiltily uncomfortable. He catches her blue eyes watching him intently when he unexpectedly looks up from his plate. Celia has her antennae quivering, on the look-out for any missed clues.

"Can I give Minerva some banana?" asks Matt, breaking into their individual musings.

"Yes, but only a half," warns William.

"I know! Otherwise you have to find the cognac –"

Matt stops in horror at his indiscretion. Celia looks at him blankly. The cognac episode happened after she'd left home. William studies his grandson's worried face but says nothing. Well done, William, say I – and oh, Matt! You will have to be more careful! He's sending me frantic messages.

"I'm sorry, *Grand-mère Kate*. What shall I say?"

"Say you need to go to the loo. At least that will get you out of the room. Quick! Go on!"

Matt makes his excuses and hastily exits the kitchen.

"Would you like some coffee, Celia?" asks William, getting up from the table.

Chapter Nineteen

I feel as though I'm in the audience in a locked cinema, watching a bad film. Nothing is going the way it should. I'd hoped that Celia and William would get together for a proper talk, either yesterday or this morning. Instead of which, William disappeared into his study, muttering something about deadlines that had to be met. Matt and Celia went for a long walk and then watched some television before having supper and going to bed. William made only the briefest of appearances all Saturday, telling them to help themselves to anything they wanted and to make themselves at home.

This morning, Sunday, William has dived back into his study, leaving Celia peeling potatoes, basting the roast and making apple crumble for lunch. Matt is deeply involved with Minerva who's never had it so good and is in seventh heaven.

There's an awful inevitability about lunch being a disaster. I know Thomas wouldn't want me to do anything to try and

187

stop Veronica's arrival but I wish she'd ring up and say she's changed her mind. When I osmose through the door into the study, my suspicions are confirmed. William is not working. He's sitting at his desk, worrying about what he should do for the best. He still hasn't made up his mind about Veronica. There's one positive thing floating around in all that worry, though. William is intrigued with Matt, whom he likes. I can't get any definite reading on what his feeling are for Celia. They seem somewhat confused. I think he may even be a little afraid of her!

They all hear Veronica's car pull up in the driveway a little after twelve. I watch her as she gets out of a brand new Audi that has all the trimmings. I must say, she and the car suit each other. She's looking as glossy as ever. In reality, she is as nervous as a cat. William appears at the front door, closely marked by Celia. I think he'd intended to have a quick word with Veronica before she came into the house but Celia has put paid to that plan.

"Hello, William!"

Veronica walks up to him and gives him a small peck on the cheek. Then she turns her attention to Celia.

"Hello, Celia! My goodness, I wouldn't have recognised you. I love the look – very ethnic.

Celia winces internally but walks forward and pre-empts a kiss on the cheek by sticking out a rigid arm in front of her so that Veronica's forced to shake her hand.

"Hello, Veronica. *You* look just as I remember."

Because I know what's going on in my daughter's head, I'm privy to the fact that she's not feeling very friendly towards her mother's old friend. Mind you, even a normal mortal would have cottoned on to that after this first exchange. The vibes coming from her bear a strong resemblance to unravelling strands of razor wire. Celia prefers to think of how she dresses not as ethnic but in a way that's individual and unique to her. She considers the other woman's high heels tarty and she thinks that, for her age, Veronica's skirt is much too short.

William leads the way back to the house, followed by Veronica and Celia taking up the rear. Once inside, they file into the kitchen where Matt is whispering to Minerva. Celia calls him over to say hello.

"Matt, this is grandfather's friend, Veronica. Come and shake hands."

He obediently walks over and shakes hands.

"*Bonjour, Madame,*" he says automatically and then realises that he should be speaking English. Veronica doesn't bat an eyelid.

"*Bonjour, Matt. Je suis enchantée de faire ta connaissance.*"

Matt smiles at her politely, then goes back to his tête-à-tête with Minerva.

Celia's looking unattractively sour. Veronica often had that effect on other women. She always did things with such unexpected flair – they just couldn't keep up with her.

William offers sherry and Celia accepts – not so Veronica.

"I'll have a good strong gin and tonic, thank you, William," she declares and then turns to my daughter on the sofa beside her. "After the twisty roads and the loose sheep and farmers out in their cars looking anywhere except at the road because they're counting the sheep that haven't yet escaped, I need something more invigorating than mere sherry."

Celia doesn't say anything. She's thinking, 'Who does she think she is? Demanding gin and tonic.'

Conversation limps along until Celia announces that lunch is ready. They gather round the table and William carves. As they eat, I'm aware that each of the adults is watching the others and trying to gauge what is going on. Talk drifts from Veronica's job to William's latest book to living in France. I feel quite embarrassed by my daughter's behaviour. She's not trying to be polite and I can't help feeling, all things considered, she owes it to her father to make an effort. She *is* staying in his house and he's being perfectly pleasant to her. Matt just keeps his head down and from time to time, posts off a question to me.

"Why is Mama cross, *Grand-mère Kate?*"

That's a difficult one.

"Perhaps she's feeling shy. She hasn't seen Miss Dillon for a long time."

"Mama is never shy," Matt telegraphs back.

Veronica is valiantly trying to keep the ball rolling. She's uncomfortably aware of Celia's blue eyes fixed on her all the time and it's getting more and more difficult for her to keep pretending that all is well. It's obvious to her that the girl suspects some sort of a liaison between her father and her mother's friend. I notice that they all manage to avoid mentioning my name.

"Tell me, Veronica," says Celia as she dishes up the apple crumble. "Do you often manage to come out here? Your job must make it difficult for you to get away from Dublin."

Veronica smiles.

"Oh, I make the occasional sortie in this direction. It's a lovely drive."

"Even with the twisty roads, absent-minded farmers and the rogue sheep?"

"Could I have some apple crumble, please, Celia?" says William.

By the end of the meal, I'm feeling like a nervous wreck. The strained atmosphere has got to Veronica and after a quick cup of coffee, she leaves. William walks with her to the car.

"This wasn't a good idea. Why did you do it?"

"Because I wanted to see you."

"You always say that! It's the excuse you make for not keeping to an agreement. You should have waited, like I asked."

"William! Why are you so frightened about Celia finding out that we're lovers?" Veronica lays a hand on his arm. "She suspects it already so what's the point in being coy?"

William ignores her hand.

"She doesn't suspect anything! Has it occurred to you that she just might be upset by her mother's death? You must realise, I don't know the girl at all and she and I have to spend some time trying to find out if any sort of a relationship between us is possible. She still resents me and having to explain about us will just make it more difficult. Can't you see that, Veronica?"

"Well, I think she should know the truth. How can she trust you, knowing that you're hiding things from her?" Veronica steps back from him. "Or is it that you simply don't want to have a relationship with *me* any longer. Is that it?"

"You're trying to push me into a corner, Veronica and I won't be pushed."

"Right! Then I'd better be getting back. Let me know if you decide you'd like to see me."

The Audi's tyres skid on the gravel as she drives off. William is not to know that just round the first bend, Veronica pulls in to the side of the road. It's a good five minutes before she feels able to continue the journey.

Just as William turns towards the house, Celia steps back from the window where she's just watched the exchange between her father and Veronica. She's outraged. What she's just seen confirms her suspicions. 'That woman,' as she thinks of Veronica, 'is having an affair with my father – and my mother only died six weeks ago.'

It's nice of her to be upset on my behalf but I wish she'd just concentrate on getting to know her father again. Anyway, she did walk out on *both* of us, so I think there's just a touch of hypocrisy in her behaviour!

With the arrogance of youth, Celia is having a go at poor William. First Veronica and now his daughter! Luckily, Matt is down by the river, looking for worms so he can go fishing.

"You're having an affair with her, aren't you?"

Celia's face is red and her voice sounds unpleasantly shrill.

William looks at her for a moment and then, very deliberately, turns away and picks up some papers from the dresser.

"I will be in my study for the rest of the afternoon. I suggest you remember that you are welcome to stay in this house until such time as you can sort out your life but please also remember that you are a guest in the home *you* once chose to leave – with all that that implies."

William walks towards his study door, leaving his daughter glaring at his back.

Celia opens her mouth to say something. I hold my breath and make a wish. She closes her mouth and starts collecting plates and glasses from the table. Thank goodness for small mercies!

I thankfully join Matt outside. He's wearing an old anorak of William's with the sleeves folded back several times and boots that are five sizes too large. I think they're the ones Celia had before she left home. Half a dozen pale worms twist around in the jamjar at his feet. His face and hands are muddy and he looks blissfully happy. He waves the jar in my direction.

"*Regarde!* I have found many worms, *Grand-mère Kate!*"

"So I see. What do you intend doing with the poor things?"

He gives me a wicked grin.

"I will get a very sharp hook and stick it into them and then I will put them on a fishing line and the fish will eat the worms and then the hook will stick into the fish. *Et, voila!*" he says, with a flourish.

"I can't help feeling sorry for the fish. I don't think being caught on a very sharp hook would be nice. It must hurt."

"You must hit the fish on the head and then they do not feel pain," my grandson says, knowledgeably.

All the same, I'm glad I'm not a fish. I don't know if it's the Irish air but Matt seems to be speaking faster and more fluently than when I first came across him. I hope he doesn't stop using a mix of French and English. At least, not when he's with the family.

193

Celia's going down to the little school in the village to see if they will take him. It's the same one that she went to so briefly as a small child. I checked it out when I arrived on Friday and I was glad to see that Miss Farringdon is no longer there. Instead, a young woman in her mid-twenties with flaming red hair, a twinkle in her eyes and a generous heart that bodes well for my grandson.

Celia has taken it upon herself to do something about my clothes. She summoned up her courage and went and tapped on William's door, earlier this afternoon.

"Would you mind if I sorted through Mum's clothes? It has to be done and it might be a good thing to get it over with."

"No, I don't mind. That's if you feel up to it. I haven't had the time," said William, looking up from his desk.

He always writes in longhand and the top of the desk is littered with pages, covered in his small, neat handwriting. Reference books stand in stacks around his chair. Celia is remembering the time she came into this room, threading her way through the piles of books; how she climbed up onto the chair and scribbled all over her father's precious manuscript. She remembers how he took her to her bedroom and spanked her and then refused to let me go to her. She gives him a cool look.

"I'll get on with it then." She hesitates and then adds, "Do you mind if I keep a few things for myself?"

William looks surprised.

"I wouldn't have thought you'd been interested in anything your mother wore. You seem to favour a more . . . unusual style of dressing."

Celia looks embarrassed.

"It's just that I don't have much money and not all that many clothes. Most of the stuff I have isn't suitable for winter in Ireland."

"Oh, I see! . . . Well, take what you want, of course."

As she leaves the room, he calls after her, "What about young Matt? Is he all right for warm clothes?"

"I've got enough to buy him what he needs, thanks."

Why does she have to be so proud and ungracious? Prickly creature that she is!

As Matt is happily dividing his time between chats with Minerva and persecuting the fish population, Celia is free to get on with the wretched clothes business. She's opened the wardrobe door and is taking down all the hangers. My daughter's thinking how dreary my clothes look. She's right – they do! I seem to have gone in for a colour range of sludge to coffee to brown. No wonder Veronica used to tear her hair over my lack of sartorial know-how.

Celia makes piles of garments on the bed. Having worked her way through the things in the wardrobe, she turns her attention to the chest-of-drawers. She's clearly unhappy at having to deal with my underclothes, which she feels are too painfully personal. Without really giving them any attention, she stuffs them all into plastic bags for the bin. I wish she would investigate a bit more thoroughly because some of it's rather pretty. One or two things Veronica gave me are positively glamorous! Not that I got round to wearing them very often. You need to have an appreciative audience for nice underwear and William hasn't seen me in a state of undress for several years.

When I had to go through my own mother's clothes, I remember being a bit shocked at finding a matching set of bright red, frilly undergarments. There was even a bright red frilly suspender belt. I remember thinking that there must have been some mistake – that they belonged to someone else. Now, I just hope that she and my father got pleasure from those skimpy bits of lace and silk. I hope that they made time for a little sauciness in an apparently mundane and respectable married life. Theirs had been a union that seemed to me to have contained no spark of fun or joy. I never saw them kiss or show affection and yet, I suppose they loved each other. I think my mother was a romantic at heart. I know she was a secret reader of novels with happy endings. I think she would have liked to be swept off her feet by a tall dark stranger. That's one thing I have in common with her – not the tall dark stranger bit – just that neither of us lived out fulfilled lives with the right partner.

There's absolutely no good in my getting maudlin and Celia hasn't discovered my few items of dashing underclothes. So she won't have the opportunity to be scandalised!

When she's finished with the clothes, she carries a small heap of the least dull jerseys and jackets over to the armchair by the window and folds the rest into dustbin bags. She's thinking 'Oxfam' and that's fine by me.

Now she turns to the drawers in my dressing-table. I never wore much make-up, so there isn't much there to interest her. I'm pleased to see her deciding to keep the clutter of spare pieces of ribbon, tubes of mascara, moisturiser and eye shadow. Then she opens the sandalwood box.

She picks up a small, tissue-wrapped bundle and tips

out the contents. The watch and gold sleepers I was wearing when I died slide onto its polished top, followed by my wedding ring. Celia's eyes fill with tears and she's thinking the 'Oh, Mum' mantra. It's a mix of 'Oh, Mum, I wish we could go back ten years and start again' and 'Oh, Mum, why did you have to go and die? I wish you were here.' Just the same as I did twenty years ago as I knelt by a heap of my own mother's clothes on *her* bedroom carpet.

It's just occurred to me that this may be the first time in years that my daughter has thought about me with affection. Why do we always make the mistake of valuing people when it's too late? I can't help thinking of all the missed chances. If we'd been better parents and if she hadn't gone away . . .

Matt bursts into the bedroom, followed by William. They are both looking pleased with themselves.

"Grandpapa has caught a fish!"

Celia looks at her father in surprise.

"Really?"

"We caught a brown trout," confirms William.

"It's enormous!" says Matt, spreading his hands in true fisherman's yarn fashion.

William laughs.

"It's about six inches long but there's no doubt about it. It's a fish."

Matt suddenly notices the pile of clothes, the plastic bags and the open box. He goes over to the dressing-table and picks up the wedding ring.

"Does this belong to *Grand-mère Kate?*"

"Put it down at once, Matthieu," snaps Celia.

She's made him jump and Matt drops it. The ring bounces and then falls flat, making a small tinkling sound.

197

"Why can I not look at her ring?" he asks, in a puzzled voice.

"Can't you see I'm in the middle of tidying Granny's things?"

William realises that she is upset. He puts a hand on Matt's shoulder and gently guides him towards the doorway.

"Come on, young man. There's something I want to show you."

As they leave the room, I hear Matt say to William, "I know *Grand-mère Kate* does not mind me looking at her things. She likes me."

My husband looks down into the boy's puzzled face and says quietly, "I'm sure she wouldn't mind. Come on! We'll talk about it later."

Chapter Twenty

For the last couple of days, I've been trying to get it into Matt's head that his new school will be nothing like the old one on the island but he's taking a lot of convincing. Although he hasn't said as much to me, what's weighing most on his mind is the possibility of being bullied.

He's trying hard to make sure that he doesn't lapse into French when he talks and quickly corrects himself each time he forgets. When Mrs Byrne comes up to the house, I see him listening, fascinated by her Wicklow accent. When she's gone home, he tries out various phrases he's heard her use – not always very successfully.

The portly, widowed Mrs Byrne is so carried away by the idea of 'looking after that poor man' that she's somehow managed to persuade William into allowing her to come up to the house for one morning a week. The fact that the poor man has an unmarried daughter and small grandson just adds to her feeling of being involved in some sort of religious crusade.

Mrs Byrne got short shrift from my daughter when she informed Celia that she ought to be taking the young one to church and she *really* should be visiting the parish priest so that Matt's preparation for confirmation can be arranged. It quite took the wind out of her sails when Celia told her that she had no intention of either of them going anywhere near the church and that the 'young one' hadn't been baptised – and that was just fine by her.

"That's desperate! You'll have to do something about that, dear," the woman exclaimed, after a shocked silence. "After all, what if something happened to him? He'd be damn –"

"I don't want to talk about this any more, Mrs Byrne, and if you mean by 'something happening to Matt,' you are saying, 'if he dies,' then he will die and he will be dead. End of story! Being baptised or anointed or whatever will not make the slightest bit of difference. Dead means dead."

How wrong can you be? I could slap her sometimes! She's as sensitive in her dealings with the people around her as a rampaging elephant in a field of sugar cane.

To give Mrs Byrne credit, Celia's rudeness hasn't made any difference in her attitude towards Matt. If anything, she's even nicer to him because she feels sorry he's been landed with such an impossible mother. Celia's behaviour gives Mrs Byrne lots to tell her neighbours down in the village.

I've promised my grandson that I will accompany him and his mother to school on his first day and then I will hang around for a while after she's left, until I'm sure everything is all right. The time has flown by and today is D-day for Matt.

Celia knows he's nervous and offers him her hand on the way down the road. Matt declines hurriedly. I can hear him thinking, 'Doesn't she *know* that's the sort of thing that will make the other boys laugh at me?'

When we arrive, the young teacher is in the small playground at the side of the building. As soon as she sees Matt and Celia, she hurries over with a welcoming smile. Tall and slim, Margaret Delaney makes Celia wish she could grow a few inches more and become gracefully willowy like the other woman. The teacher shakes hands with my daughter.

"Hello, nice to see you again, Miss Fitzgerald. So this is Matt! Hi there! I'm Miss Delaney. Come on and I'll introduce you to the others. They're dying to meet you."

I can see Celia is happy to leave Matt with her and even he looks as though he thinks things might not be as bad as he feared.

All the same, he still sends out a silent, "Don't go yet, *Grand-mère Kate!*"

"No, I promised I'd stick around until you see that it's all going to be fine," I reassure him.

After a few minutes, he's chatting away to a group of children as though he hasn't a worry in the world.

"All right if I go now, Matt?" I ask.

"Yes, yes! You can go!"

William has decided that he must try and have a proper talk with Celia. When she gets back from taking Matt to school, he's waiting for her in the kitchen with a pot of fresh coffee and a plate of custard creams. He's dredged up the memory of her liking them as a child. My husband is nervous of saying the wrong thing to his difficult daughter but he bravely gets the ball rolling.

"I think it's time you and I had a proper conversation."

Celia's instinct is to turn round and walk out of the room. The idea of having a heart-to-heart with her father seriously alarms her. I wait anxiously while she hesitates. William sensibly doesn't give her a chance to turn and run.

"Don't look like a frightened deer. We can't let old wrongs ruin the present – and the future. Sit down and talk to me, if only for Matt's sake."

Unwillingly, Celia sits. William pours her a cup of coffee and offers her the plate of custard creams. She looks at them with mild surprise.

"You remembered!"

"How could I not? Your mother never forgot the time when you were recovering from measles. You hadn't eaten anything solid for days and suddenly there you were, sitting up in bed, demanding custard creams. We tried explaining that we'd run out but you weren't having any of it. You cried so bitterly, I had to go down to the village shop and beg Eugene to open up so that I could buy a packet."

Celia can't help smiling.

"I must have been a right pain."

"Sometimes. Just a little."

A silence and then Celia asks, "Why were you so strict with me when I was growing up?"

"Because I didn't know any better. You were our first and, as it turned out, our only child. I had had no brothers or sisters of my own and I'd no yardstick. I thought that by being strict I was doing you a favour – that you would thank me later on." He hesitates and then says something so unexpected that

Celia's defensive expression starts to fade a little. "Instead of which, I made your mother unhappy and drove you away."

My daughter is blessedly silent. Celia had thought at the start of the conversation that William was going to have a go at her – and now, she doesn't know what to say. She feels she should find some way to reciprocate his frankness.

Tentatively, she asks, "Do you know why I didn't send you and Mum my address in France?"

"Your mother felt that it was because you were still angry with us."

"No, it wasn't just that. I was ashamed. That's why I didn't let you know where I was."

"Ashamed? Ashamed of what? Not of Matt, I hope?"

"I was ashamed of being stupid enough to be taken in by Matt's father and of becoming pregnant. I thought you and Mum would be so disappointed. Especially you." She looks down at her hands, lying uneasily in her lap. "I was convinced that what had happened would confirm all your worst suspicions about me."

"Didn't it cross your mind that we would have wanted to help. Yes, of course we would have been upset to learn what had happened but we would have supported you. Can you imagine how much your mother would have wanted you to come home so that she could make a fuss of you? The way you left hurt her dreadfully."

"Don't!" Celia shouts. "I'm sorry! I didn't mean it to come out like that. I loved Mum and I knew she loved me. The awful thing is, I knew it and I still went ahead and hurt her." She stares straight at William. "I was sure that *you* didn't love me though. Nothing Mum and I did was ever good enough for you."

The bitterness in her voice hits home but he manages to hide his discomfort.

"Well, all I can say is that I do love you and now your mother's gone, I've come to realise that I should have made more of an effort in many areas."

"But you never loved her, did you?"

William's answer is courageous.

"No, I didn't. I was flattered that she seemed to like me when we first met. I did your mother a great disservice by marrying her."

"But you're in love with Veronica?"

"I'm not sure what being in love involves. If it means I enjoy her company and would like to spend more time with her . . . if it means that she helps me forget my troubles and worries and makes me laugh . . . if being in love means that I don't want her to come to any harm and that I miss her when she's not here, then perhaps you could say that I am."

"Does she love you?"

"She tells me she does."

Celia doesn't say anything for a few minutes. She's trying hard to digest all this new information. My daughter's also attempting to come to terms with a different father to the one she imagined she'd known and always disliked so much. When she does speak, her voice is quieter.

"Were you . . . close to Veronica before Mum died?"

For a second, William considers not telling the truth, but only for a second.

"Yes, I was. For quite a long time before."

"Did Mum know?"

"I don't think so. I hope not."

Celia tries, unsuccessfully, to keep a critical tone from

creeping in to her voice. "She would *never* have done anything like that to you."

Without hesitation, William replies, "No, of course she wouldn't."

I am high above the house in the glen and Thomas's comforting presence is with me.

"What's the matter? Kate?"

"I feel like crying. I've just seen a William I have never known – even though I lived with him for nearly thirty years. A man who can be kind and compassionate. Veronica told him about Milo. He could so easily have said something to Celia just now. Why did it take my death for him to show himself as he really is – and for me to see?"

"Don't blame yourself too much, Kate. William has changed a lot since your death."

"Everyone seems to be changing."

"How are they changing, Kate?"

"For the better, it seems!"

"Then, girl, rejoice and be glad, as the good book says!" Thomas sounds amused at my humours. Suddenly he adds, "I have noticed a tendency in you to take things too seriously. Do you like to dance, Kate?"

"I've never really danced! I was hopeless at dancing as a teenager and William refused to go anywhere near a dance floor. Why?"

"You will dance, girl. You wait and see! Now I must be going. I will be back for you in a while. You can't remain in your present state forever, my dear Kate," he says enigmatically – and is gone.

I'm left feeling troubled. I've no time to waste. I realise

that I'd drifted into a condition in which I thought I had all the time in the world. It seems as if that commodity is not as open-ended as I imagined; at least, not in this dimension.

Miss Delaney has come up to the house at the end of Matt's first week at school. When Celia opens the door to her, of course her first thought is that something's wrong.

"Is Matt all right?"

"Oh, he's just fine! Settling in like a dream. They've all gone for a nature walk with Mr Friel so I took this opportunity to pop in for a chat – if you have the time?"

"Of course. Come in."

They sit down together on the kitchen sofa. Celia offers coffee.

"No, thanks. I can't stay for too long. This is lovely!" comments Miss Delaney, holding her hands up to the open fire that is crackling and shooting sparks from the burning logs. "It's just that I wanted to ask you a bit more about Matt. He's doing so well. The other children like him and he's had no trouble making friends. He's so obedient and polite in class. The rest of them could take a leaf out of his book." She laughs. "I've noticed that he's incredibly artistic too – quite out of the ordinary, in fact. I expect you know all about that already. What I am concerned about is his reading. I know you said that he had a problem in that area. It is possible that your Matt may be suffering from some form of dyslexia."

After Miss Delaney has gone, William comes into the kitchen and finds Celia still sitting in front of the fire, looking upset.

"What's the matter? I heard you talking to Matt's teacher just now. You look as though she's given you some bad news."

"She has. She seems to think that Matt is suffering from some sort of reading disorder and that he should go and be tested."

"Well, I'm impressed," says William. "It didn't take her long to pick up on that. She must be good at her job. So, why are you looking so glum?"

"I thought that Matt not being good at reading was just part of the way he was – because of his father and the bullying at school and all that sort of thing. I thought he just needed some sort of counselling. I didn't realise that it might be something more serious. It's all very well for her to say that I should take him to be tested. How can I afford to take him to a specialist?"

"I'll arrange all that."

"Why should you?" Celia snaps, with all her old tact and sensitivity.

"Because that's the sort of thing grandpapas do for their grandchildren," says William, with a slight smile.

He really is learning! Once again, he's succeeded in silencing our daughter.

William's being splendid! He's booked Matt into some place where they specialise in his sort of problem. He's explained all about it to his grandson in a simple, low-key way and Matt can't wait to go to his first appointment.

Although my husband appears to be taking all this in his stride, he's not finding it easy. Before nearly every action and word involving Celia, he's monitoring what he's doing or saying. He's frightened of making a mistake, of alienating Matt or bringing a halt to the slow but visible thaw in Celia's attitude towards him.

I look at my daughter with her silver studs, her spiky hair and Indian skirts and blouses – spoilt by having to wear one of my thick cardigans over them. It would be so nice if she could only be a little more generous-spirited. Then I remember her childhood. Some things just can't be rushed, I suppose.

Celia's not happy and that doesn't surprise me. She keeps telling herself that François was bad for her, that what he did was cruel and wrong and that she's well out of an impossible situation. However, that doesn't seem to stop her lying awake each morning before daylight, chewing it all over in her mind and feeling lonely and miserable. She doesn't know what she feels about her father or how to behave towards him.

Celia's still feeling guilty about me. I wish I could give her a gentle shake and remind her that she wasn't responsible for my cancer or my 'falling off the perch', as Matt likes to call my death. Now, there's this new problem with her son and his reading. She keeps forgetting that Matt's not over-worried about it. That young man is too busy enjoying his new school and newfound friends to worry about anything too much at the moment!

In fact, Matt's been so occupied with his new life, that he's hardly had the time to talk to me much lately. I manage to nab him after tea today and suggest a walk along the river.

"I must ask Mama," he says, dashing along the passage to Celia's darkened room.

She has a headache and is lying down, eyes closed, doing her best to meditate. I never tried meditation but Celia's version seems a bit hit-and-miss. I think what she's trying to do is relax each part of her body, bit by bit. Each time she succeeds in making one part go soft and floppy, the previous bit seems to seize up again. When she's achieved the miracle of all-over floppiness, she's meant to visualise an idyllic place and imagine herself in the middle of it, smelling the flowers and hearing the birds twitter. However, every time my poor daughter chooses her idea of a heavenly place, François seems to invade it. Sometimes it is the hard faces of the island women that appear in the middle of a forest glade or a tropical beach. These are the ones who used to talk in front of her about what a disgrace she was, getting herself pregnant etc. etc. I can't help wondering if she mightn't be better off forgetting the meditation for a while and going for a brisk walk with Matt in the fresh air.

"Mama? Can I go down to the river for a little while?"

Celia raises her head from the pillow and turns to look at him.

"Yes, you can but don't go anywhere near the edge of the bank. It's not safe. There's been a lot of rain and the river's very full. Be back in half-an-hour. OK?"

"OK!" he says, happily.

He runs back to the kitchen and slips into William's old anorak. It takes him a while to get the zip done up but he manages. Then he puts on a pair of smart new yellow Wellingtons that Celia bought him last week.

"I am ready, *Grand-mère Kate*. Let's go!"

We walk side by side along the muddy path that runs close

to the fast-running river that winds from the head of the valley to the village. Matt is in a perpetual state of wonderment. Because of his enjoyment of this new world in which he finds himself, I find I'm looking at it all in a fresh light. It's almost as though a filmy layer has been scraped away from my eyes. His enjoyment is infectious.

"Look, *Grand-mère Kate!* There are some deers on the mountain over there."

A herd of deer is moving swiftly through the heather from one patch of forestry to another. As we walk, Matt keeps making quick sorties into the sallies that border the path. The bracken is brown and friable after the October frosts and it crackles as he tramples around in the undergrowth. Suddenly he stops, turning his head from side to side, sniffing the air like a small animal.

"What is that funny smell?" he asks.

A great waft of pungent musk fills the air.

"It's a fox, Matt. There are a lot of them in the valley. When I first came to live here, there was one who became so tame he'd come right up to the back door for scraps of food. I used to call him Ruadh, like the valley. He was very handsome."

Rounding the next bend, Matt comes to an abrupt halt.

"Look at that strange bird! He has only one leg!"

A large heron is standing like a statue beside a spit of gravel.

"That's a heron. The other leg is tucked away, having a rest. He's like you and Grandpapa. He likes to do a spot of fishing but in his case, he doesn't need a sharp hook. Look how pointed the end of his beak is."

We watch the heron for a couple of minutes as Matt

wants to see the bird in action but the heron just stands there, the wind slightly ruffling his head feathers. After a while my grandson walks quietly past so as not to disturb him.

After the next bend, we come to a wooden bridge, joining the two banks. It's been made by the men who work for the forestry department and consists of slim pine-trunks, lashed together with wire. Because of all the heavy rain over the last week, the water is boiling and rushing along only inches away from the bottom of the bridge. Matt picks up some twigs and walks to the middle. He peers over the rail at the noisy water below.

"Why is the water brown, *Grand-mère Kate?*"

"That water comes from high up in the mountains, far away from the top of the valley. It flows through the turf bogs and that's why it looks brown but it's very clean and pure."

Matt drops one of the twigs into the water and watches it bob and twirl as it careers downstream.

"I will throw in two sticks. One for you and one for me and we shall see who gets to that tree first," he says, pointing at a small birch on the river's edge.

So, until his supply runs out, we try and guess whose stick will win. All the time, my grandson talks and asks the never-ending questions which I never tire of answering. Then I remember Celia's directive for him to be back at the end of half-an-hour.

"Matt, remember what your mum said. I think we should go home now. It's just starting to get dark."

Reluctantly, he lets go of the slippery rail and climbs down to the path, giving a last look over his shoulder at the bridge.

On our way back to the house, I see pale shapes watching us

from the shadow of distant trees. I'm too happy answering my grandson's questions to take much notice of them. It just strikes me in passing that even from afar, they have a melancholy feel to them.

As we near the steep path up to the house, I ask, "Do you like it here, Matt?"

"I like it here very much, *Grand-mère Kate*. It is . . . it is great!"

I smile to myself. In no time at all, he'll sound just like the rest of the children at his school.

Chapter Twenty-one

It's Sunday and Celia's gone off to Dublin to see some old schoolfriends. I hope she comes back a little more cheerful than she's been lately. It's been like having a small, angry thundercloud rolling round the place. Her father does his best but ends up taking refuge in his study whenever he can. Matt's too busy to spend time analysing his mother's mood-swings.

William has lit the fire in the small sitting-room that opens off the kitchen and he and Matt are playing Monopoly. Minerva's furious! She hates it when people use that room. It means she can't see what's going on and she feels left out of things. My offer to keep her company was turned down with a muttered, "Bugger!"

After William has bankrupted Matt while trying his best not to, he pushes the board to one side and looks at his grandson, who's gone to stand by the window. He's watching a wren foraging among the autumn leaves.

"Matt, there's something I wanted to ask you."

Matt turns and looks over to where William is sitting, peering at him over the top of his glasses.

"Yes, Grandpapa?"

"How do you know about the time Minerva was ill and your grandmother gave her cognac?"

Matt's suddenly looking desperately uncomfortable. I haven't been concentrating too much on the conversation up until now. I was dozing, enjoying the layer of hot air lying trapped below the ceiling. I swoop down, not at all sure of the best way of handling the situation. Before I've time to come up with a suggestion, Matt's waded in with both feet. For some reason, he's decided to try the truth out on his grandfather.

"Do you believe in ghosts, Grandpapa?"

William senses that if he admits he doesn't, then the conversation might be at an end. So he decides to do his best to go along with the idea.

"I suppose it's possible they exist."

He can see that Matt is having difficulty over what to say next so he waits patiently.

"I know a ghost." Matt searches his grandfather's face for signs of disbelief or ridicule. William's features however, are composed into 'serious listening' mode. "It is *Grand-mère Kate*," says my grandson, with a flourish.

This should be interesting! Matt's concentrating so hard on William that I think it's best I don't do anything to complicate things for the moment. I unobtrusively retire into the corner behind the turf basket.

"Is it?" says William, gravely. "Do you see her very often?"

"Yes! All the time."

"Don't tell him I'm in the room, for goodness' sake," I hiss at him from the shadows. "It might make him nervous."

Matt sends out a quick 'OK' and then turns his attention back to William.

"*Grand-mère Kate* is my friend and she helped me when Didier and Claude bullied me at the school."

"Your grandmother was with you in France?"

"Yes!"

"How did she help you?"

Matt giggles and his face takes on the sort of look that a person has when he or she's remembering someone else's well merited and undignified comeuppance.

"She made Claude hit Didier and then she made Didier push Claude and after, she made them eat weeds and put mud on their faces. It was great!"

'Great' seems to be Matt's favourite newly learned expression just at the moment. It's obvious from William's thoughts that he's taken aback at how certain Matt is that he's seen my ghost. 'Only to be expected after all the poor lad's been through,' is what he's thinking. He comes to the conclusion that perhaps it would be a good thing not to encourage his young grandson with his fantasies.

"What you've told me is very interesting, Matt, but . . ."

Matt interrupts him with, "And you know what was the best thing that *Grand-mère Kate* did? She told me what the house here looked like so I could paint it and then when Mama saw the picture, it made her think of coming to Ireland. It was all *Grand-mère Kate's* idea or we would not be here," he says, darting a triumphant glance in my direction.

"Sorry, Matt, you've rather lost me. Your grandmother

got you to paint a picture of *this* house when you hadn't seen it – not even in a photograph?"

"Yes! And she learned me to do up my buttons and tie my shoes too!"

This is all getting a bit much for my poor husband. He hasn't a clue what to say next. He thinks that he'd better have a word with Celia about it all – especially the bit about the painting. If he did paint a picture of the house, Matt *must* have seen a photo of it first.

"Well, that's very interesting. What would you like to do now? Go and have a chat with Minerva?"

"OK!"

Leaving William in the sitting-room to ponder the recent revelations, Matt goes into the kitchen and over to Minerva's cage. The bird does her ritual welcome shuffle that was once reserved only for me – but I don't mind in the least!

As my grandson thoughtfully scratches the back of her neck, he whispers, "I don't think Grandpapa believes me, *Grand-mère Kate*."

"Well, most grown-up don't believe in ghosts, do they? When I was alive, I don't think I did. It's nothing to be disappointed about but perhaps it's better not to talk about it to other people. Perhaps it's best kept as our secret – just yours and mine."

Matt nods in agreement but I can tell that he's disappointed.

My grandson is safely tucked up in bed. William's pleased to see that the trip to Dublin seems to have done Celia good. She's not particularly informative but at least the pall of gloom has lifted a bit. They've eaten an omelette and watched the nine o'clock news on the telly.

"More wine?" asks William.

She holds out her glass.

"Thanks. How was Matt this afternoon? I hope he was good."

As William switches off the telly, he's wondering how best to broach the subject of Matt's preoccupation with the spirit world.

"He was very well behaved. You should be proud of yourself – he's a nice boy, Celia. There's just one thing that worries me a little though . . ."

"What? His reading? I thought that wasn't something to worry about. You said it will all sort itself out with the right help."

" . . . It will. If you just let me finish what I was saying. I'm concerned about his rather over-fertile imagination. Has he ever talked to you about seeing . . . ghosts?"

"No!" Celia laughs. "Why? Did he tell you he had?"

"Yes, he did and not just any old ghost either. Matt says he has regular chats with your mother."

Celia's smile fades.

"But that's just mad! Someone must have been telling him fairy stories. Mrs Byrne's got a typical countrywoman's over-active imagination. Perhaps she's responsible."

"I don't know. He says it started when you were living in France. Apparently, he painted a picture of this house from a description given to him by your mother."

"He *did* do a painting. I recognised the house straight away." Celia's voice sounds odd. "It was an exact likeness and I never managed to find out how he did it. I hadn't got

217

any photos of the place with me. When I tried to find out, he clammed up and all he would say was that it was 'magic'." She looks appalled and puts a hand up to her face. "Oh, my God! I saw him a couple of times behaving as though he was having an animated conversation with someone who just wasn't there. He was waving his arms around and laughing." Then she remembers the wretched incident with the ball. "Do you think there's something dreadfully wrong with him – some sort of psychiatric problem?"

Celia's looking really distressed now and William's wishing that he'd just kept his worries to himself.

"No, I don't think there's anything wrong with Matt – apart from mild dyslexia. Calm down! There's always a rational explanation for this sort of thing. Perhaps you had a photo when you first arrived there and you've forgotten or it's possible that you'd described the house in great detail at some point. Whatever the answer, you can be sure that there is one. Don't get all upset. It won't help Matt keep his feet on the ground. The best thing to do is to make life as normal as possible for him – ignore any wild fantasies he may have. He'll grow out of them soon enough."

Poor William is trying his best to persuade himself that there's nothing to worry about in Matt's strange behaviour. At the same time, he's attempting to comfort Celia. It doesn't cross his mind for a moment that I'm not just a figment of his grandson's imagination. He refills both their wine glasses.

"We might as well finish the bottle. Drink up and cheer up!"

Celia gives him a woeful imitation of a smile.

Oh, dear! I think Matt's idea of making a clean breast of things has rather backfired. I shall have to remind him to keep me under wraps. Wicked old Minerva's not given the game away so I'm sure he can be just as discreet if he puts his mind to it.

As I do each night, I slip into Matt's room to make sure all's well. He's dreaming about the bridge over the river and he's playing some sort of stepping game on the lichen-spotted stones near the bridge. I'm just about to tune out of his dream when I see something I don't like. My grandson's not alone. There are others standing on the slippery stones that rear out of the tumbling brown water – thin, miserable-looking figures. I thought he hadn't noticed them when we walked home in the twilight the other evening. I wasn't even sure if he would be able to see them. I was obviously wrong. I don't know who those skeleton shapes belong to but I know that I don't like them. They make me feel strangely afraid.

During the past weeks, when Matt was having a bad nightmare, I'd insert into his dream my idea of the sort of thing that would make him happy. Tonight, I have fun, conjuring up a silver-suited spaceman attached by a silver umbilical cord to a fantastical gold space ship. The gleaming figure is dancing and looping the loop in a black sky and down below, the green and blue earth spins silently. St Exupéry would be proud of me! When he looks carefully, Matt can see that the man in the silver space suit is none other than himself. He smiles contentedly and turns over.

I've just got back from accompanying a cheerful Matt down to his school. It looks as though Celia might give some music lessons there. Miss Delaney was delighted to find that Matt's mother plays the flute and said that quite a few of the national schools in neighbouring villages might be interested if she'd be prepared to give recorder classes.

Celia's not being terribly enthusiastic about the idea but she knows perfectly well she has to find a way to start earning money. William refuses to let her go on the dole.

"There's absolutely no need. You have a home here. Leave the dole for people who really need it," he said, firmly.

For a moment, Celia thought about arguing with him and then decided against it. Perhaps she's learning some sense!

When Matt gets back for his lunch, there's a large, square parcel waiting for him beside his place setting on the kitchen table. His face lights up.

"What is in the packet, Mama?"

"I don't know. Your grandfather must have put it there when I wasn't looking."

Matt looks at William, who's busy feeding the fire with more logs.

"What is it, Grandpapa?"

"Why don't you open it and see?" suggests William, standing up and brushing wood dust off his rather baggy corduroy trousers – that he's had for years.

Matt tears off the wrapping and out fall a cascade of tubes of oil paint, brushes and pad. He looks at them in amazement. Slowly, his expression turns from curiosity to delight. Almost shyly, he goes over to the fire, where my husband is standing watching him.

"Grandpapa, thank you very much. It is a beautiful gift. The first painting I will make is for you."

I can tell that William's chuffed to bits.

All he comes out with though is, "Glad you like it. Right! We'd better have some lunch. I'm sure this young man's starving!"

All through the meal, Matt's eyes keep wandering over to the paints, now sitting on the table under one of the windows. His thoughts are full of questions about what he should paint. While Celia and her father are talking, Matt asks me what I think should be the subject of his first oil painting.

"Just look out of the windows, Matt. There are so many lovely things just waiting for you to paint them. When you get back from school this afternoon, walk around outside a little and see if you can make up your mind which view you like best."

"Great! I will do that," he telepaths back.

When lunch is over, Matt puts on his jacket and goes over to say goodbye to Minerva. Meanwhile, Celia, who's been simmering for the last twenty minutes, opens the dishwasher door with unnecessary force and starts dropping knives and forks into it as though she's practising for a javelin-throwing contest. When Matt's gone, she rounds on William.

"Tell me! Are you trying to buy his affection?"

William slowly replaces the plates he's carrying back on to the table.

"What on earth do you mean by that extraordinary remark, Celia?"

"I don't ever remember you buying *me* presents. Are you trying to make up for it by being generous to Matt?"

My husband stares at her for a moment and then says in a quiet voice, "No, I'm not trying to 'buy' Matt's affection. I think he and I like each other well enough without my having to resort to that sort of ploy. The reason you don't remember me buying you presents is probably because your mother was so much better than I was at choosing the sort of things you liked. She enjoyed shopping for you. Also, I was working away from home for quite a lot of the time."

Celia suddenly plonks herself down on the arm of the sofa and bursts into tears.

"I'm so sorry, Dad! I don't know why I say the things I do sometimes. I just blurt stuff out before I've had time to think properly. It's just that I haven't ever had enough money to buy Matt the things he would like. I feel such a failure."

William goes and stands beside her. He doesn't know how best to console his daughter. After dithering for a minute, he pats her awkwardly on the shoulder a couple of times.

"Do you realise that's the first time you've called me 'Dad' since you came home?" Celia doesn't reply but she's listening. "And what makes you think you're a failure?"

"I just feel that . . . every time I'm faced with having to make a decision, I always seem to come up with the wrong answer. I just don't think I'm a very good mother to Matt."

"Well, if it makes you feel any better, I don't think I was a very good father but I'm doing my best to improve my performance. You're not going to stop trying, are you?"

Celia looks up at him. Her face is all damp and shiny.

To me, she looks like a child of sixteen – not a twenty-six-year-old parent.

"Of course not!"

"Well, as far as I can see, that's what matters – to keep on trying."

At this juncture, Minerva, who's been quiet for some time, seems to suddenly awake, phoenix-like, from a deep sleep. She stands on tiptoe, shakes herself and then peers over at the two people by the fire to make quite sure she has an audience.

"*Sacré bleu!*" she shrieks, at the top of her voice.

William turns round in astonishment.

"Did I hear what I thought I heard?"

Celia's begun to laugh uncontrollably.

"The bloody parrot's started talking French!"

"Now I know what Matt's been teaching her during all their get-togethers! That boy's not quite as innocent as he looks," comments William, joining in her laughter.

As far as I'm concerned, the day's ended on a good note. After Matt had done his little bit of homework, he got out his new paints. He seemed unusually quiet and thoughtful. I've had strict instructions not to look at what he's decided to do.

"I want to give you a surprise, *Grand-mère Kate*. So it is forbidden to look." Then he adds, "You must not look at my thoughts either. Promise?"

I promised. I haven't any idea what he's chosen as his subject but he spent a long time before he picked up his brush, just gazing out of the window with a slight frown. He wasn't able to wander around outside, looking at things like

I'd suggested because it rained heavily all afternoon. It hasn't stopped yet. Even with the windows closed, you can hear the roar of the river in flood.

While Matt painted, William worked in his study. He's nearly finished his book – something to do with the Reformation – and he seems pleased with it. When I watch him writing at his desk now, he seems much more content than I ever remember him being, in spite of his missing Veronica.

She's the reason I'm feeling pleased about today. Well, Celia's the reason really but it concerns Veronica. I've just overheard a telephone conversation that I wouldn't have believed possible only a few days ago. Celia rang her! Rather diffidently, she asked Veronica if she was going to drop in during the coming week. There was a long pause.

"Excuse me for saying this, Celia, but I got the impression last time I was there that you couldn't wait to see the back of me."

"Well . . . since you left, Dad and I've done a bit of talking."

"Good! Glad to hear it! I'm sure there was a lot for you to discuss. I don't see how that alters your attitude to me though."

"Dad told me that you and he'd been having an affair . . . for quite a long time . . . even before Mum died."

Another pause and then, "He talked about him and me?"

"Yes."

"I see! I didn't think he was going to say anything. I also thought that he felt the same way as you – that he really didn't want me around."

"No, that's not true. I think he's missing you . . . a lot. I think he's been lonely. Although he'd never say as much to me. Would it be possible for you to come and see him one day soon?"

"I'm not going to give you an answer right now. I'm not sure if it would be a good idea or not but . . . thank you for ringing, Celia. It was nice of you."

I feel rather proud of my daughter! I know just how difficult it was for her to make that phone call. It seems that she's started to consider William's welfare and is not spending all her time, floundering around in circles, worrying about her own problems. I find that enormously cheering!

Chapter Twenty-two

After three days, the rain has finally stopped and a watery-looking sun's struggled out from behind the clouds and turned the mountain opposite a pale yellow. The sound of the river roaring as it tumbles over the granite rocks below the house is even louder than before.

Matt doesn't seem to take any notice of bad weather. As soon as he gets back from school and his homework is done, then out come the paints. He's shut himself in the small sitting-room and he's painting away now. I'm finding it quite difficult to stay out – but a promise is a promise. I'll just have to be patient! William's also finding it hard not to take a peep at the work in progress. So far he's managed to hold back.

Celia was thrilled when he suggested yesterday that she should have my car, which has been sitting in the garage for the past six months.

"Are you sure? I haven't driven since I left home but my licence will be OK until some time in the summer."

"I'll arrange with the insurance company to have it transferred into your name."

So, Celia's going to be the new owner of Reliable Renée, my five-year-old, bottle-green Renault. The idea of being mobile has brought a sparkle to her eye.

"I'll be able to take Matt out to see the countryside. He'll love that!"

Matt, however, is not the least bit interested in jaunting around the countryside at the moment. Apart from the occasional confab with Minerva, his painting is taking up every spare minute of his day – and his thoughts. For the first time since I've known him, he's blocking me from getting into his mind. It usually only happens while he's painting. I suppose it's because he knows I like to see what he's thinking and he's afraid if he lets me in, the painting won't be a surprise any more. Today, he was untypically moody. When I suggested going for a walk together to enjoy some mountain air and the fact that it had stopped raining, he turned me down almost abruptly and pulled down his mental shutters.

So, I've left him to it! He'll be his usual self soon, I expect. I think I'll check out how Celia is. She announced at lunchtime that she was going to spring-clean the car, inside and out.

"Why do you say 'spring-clean' when tomorrow is the first day of November?" asked Matt, with annoying logic.

Celia couldn't think of anything better to say than, "Because you just *do*. That's all!"

She's got the hose out and is rinsing away the spider's webs from around the wing mirrors. It always amused me the way, each time I'd use the car, I'd wipe away its handiwork and there would be never any sign of the spider itself in or on the car. Then, when I went to take it out again, there was always a fresh web decorating the mirror. Its owner must have been lurking behind the glass. I wonder if it enjoyed travelling over the bumpy Wicklow roads at forty miles an hour!

Celia's just got round to hosing down the hubcaps when there's a sound rather like an old-fashioned sewing machine and a Volkswagen pulls up at the gate. A tall man with dark, curly hair comes to the entrance and looks over to where Celia's working. He looks slightly surprised, as if he were expecting someone else to be in the driveway, washing the car.

His face is somehow familiar. Suddenly, I experience a feeling of panic. Of course I should recognise him. It's Milo! He looks older and more weathered than when I last saw him but he has the same easy way of walking and he's still as thin as a lath. *Now* what do I do? More to the point – what on earth is he doing here? He promised when we said goodbye that he wouldn't ever come back.

Celia doesn't hear his footsteps on the gravel because of the noise of water, gushing out of the hose. She doesn't see him coming either because she's bending down with her back to him. He walks up close to her and when he speaks, she jumps as though she's been bitten.

"Hello! Am I in the right place? I was looking for a Mrs Fitzgerald – Mrs Kate Fitzgerald."

Celia hurriedly turns off the hose and, apart from a blackbird singing, all is quiet. She's wondering what this rather good-looking man wants and why he's enquiring after her mother.

"She doesn't live here any more . . . I mean . . . my mother's dead."

She's not prepared for the anguished look that appears on Milo's face. It takes a moment for what Celia's just said to sink in and then he lets out a sound that is almost a groan.

"Oh, no! She can't be!"

Celia, thinking he might be some sort of lunatic, takes a step back and stares at him.

"Well, I'm afraid she is. May I ask who you are?"

When he answers her, his voice has a slight shake in it.

"I'm sorry! My name's Milo Rowntree. I did some garden work for your mother one summer, a few years back."

"I see. Well, my name's Celia."

She's still keeping her distance but I can see that my daughter's intrigued. Milo's still looking very shaken. His colour hasn't come back yet and it makes his six o'clock shadow stand out, blue-black, against his sallow skin.

He asks, "Are you Kate's . . . her only daughter?"

"Yes," says Celia, cagily. "Why do you ask?"

"It's just that when I was working for your mother, she was very upset about a missing daughter who'd left home the previous year. I suppose that must have been you."

"I suppose it must," Celia replies.

I can see that she's none too pleased to hear that this stranger knows about her causing me distress. It's not the sort of thing that one would want a person to know about you when you first meet them.

Oh, Lord! Things are going from bad to worse. William's just joined them in the driveway.

"Is there a problem?" he asks Celia, glancing at the tall man standing beside the car.

"Dad, this is Milo Rowntree. He says he did some work in the garden for Mum one summer. Do you remember him?"

William stiffens slightly. The two men look at each other. A warning bell is clanging so hard in my husband's head, I'm surprised the clapper doesn't fly off.

"No, I'm afraid I don't remember. I think I may have been away at the time."

Milo's looking a little better now. He'd obviously prepared himself for a possible confrontation with my husband but not for the news of my death. He steps forward, hand outstretched.

"Hello, Mr Fitzgerald. Milo Rowntree. I'm sorry to land out of the blue on you like this. I hadn't heard about Mrs Fitzgerald's death, I'm afraid. I'm so sorry."

William gives his hand a minimal shake and then quickly lets go. Instead of exchanging a few sentences and then sending him on his way, my husband decides to invite Milo inside. And he accepts!

William signals to Celia behind Milo's back that she can get on with washing the car. My daughter's dying to come inside with them but, instead, she turns the hose on again with a ferocious frown.

William offers Milo some tea.

"Make yourself comfortable. I won't be a moment. The kettle's only just boiled."

While William gets out mugs and makes the tea, Milo looks around the room. I see him glance in the direction of the passage leading to the spare room – now Matt's. He studies William's thinning hair and slightly stooped back and he's thinking, 'So this is Kate's husband! The man who never made her happy. Poor, unloved Kate, whom I had to see just once to make sure she was all right, even though I promised not to come back. It seems impossible that she's not still here.' I quickly tune out of his thoughts. I don't really want to know what's in his mind. My concern is for William. Will he use the information given to him by Veronica and face Milo with it or will he decide that he doesn't want to know for certain. After all, what can be gained by his being sure that this still young man was once his wife's lover?

William carries the mugs over to the table and pushes one in Milo's direction. I notice he doesn't go as far as offering him a biscuit.

"What brings you in our direction? As I've never seen you around, I presume you don't live in this part of the world," says William, trying to keep his voice sounding casual.

"I live in Dublin. I've just landed a job in UCD as a lecturer. After being abroad for the last six or seven years, I thought it would be good to visit some of the old haunts."

"I see! You wanted to visit old haunts, did you?" William gives Milo one of his short, sharp glances over the top of his glasses – the kind that used to unnerve me so much. It's funny, but they wouldn't frighten me now and Milo doesn't seem at all put out.

William continues to quiz him, "What's your subject?"

"I'm attached to the Geology department. I'm a clay mineralogist but I've a special interest in sediments."

231

"Interesting!" says William.

His tone shows that he finds Milo's chosen subject deadly dull.

"I remember Ka . . ." Milo stumbles and then continues, "Mrs Fitzgerald saying that you were a writer."

"I think, given the circumstances, you could call my wife by her first name, don't you?" There is a moment of deafening silence before William continues, "Yes, I write books. My daughter once described them as 'boring tomes about religious freaks'. I'm sure quite a few people would agree with her."

William smiles slightly at no one in particular.

This is ghastly! They both sit there, drinking their tea, eyeing one another, each one wondering what to say next. From reading William's mind, he's thinking he'd like to take out a cudgel and bludgeon Milo over the head with it. Milo's determined not to allow himself to be either patronised or bullied.

William's just about to ask him what the work was that he did in the garden that summer when Celia makes a timely – as far as I'm concerned – entrance. Her curiosity's got the better of her and the desire to find out what's being said by the two men in the kitchen has finally become overwhelming.

I see Milo watching her with interest as she crosses the room. My daughter's not looking her best. She's wearing a pair of dungarees, rolled up at the leg and an old and shapeless mohair sweater that I used to put on when I felt unwell and needed to snuggle into something soft and comforting. I notice there's also a large hole in the toe of her left sock. She's wearing odd socks too!

"I've finished the car," she announces in a bright voice, ignoring the irritated expression on her father's face. "Is that a freshly made pot?" She feels the side of the teapot. "Good, I'm dying for a cuppa. I'll see if Matt wants anything." She goes over to the closed sitting-room door and knocks. "Matt, I won't come in and spy but would you like to come out and have a drink of something?" Getting no answer, Celia opens the door a crack and peers in. She suddenly pushes the door wide and says, "Matt?" She turns to William. "Dad, where's Matt?"

I suddenly have a presentiment that something is most dreadfully wrong.

William, alerted, gives Celia a worried glance and says, "He was in there, painting up until an hour ago then I think he went outside. He's probably in the garden somewhere. Do you want me to go and check?"

"No, I'll go."

While Celia is looking for Matt, I make my way as quickly as I can into the sitting-room. His finished painting is lying on the small table under the window. As I study it, my feelings of unease multiply tenfold.

In meticulous detail, Matt has painted the wooden bridge over the river. The water is a raging torrent – the colour of burnt amber, laced with curling swirls of white foam – almost covering the stones. He has captured the feeling of a misty autumn evening beautifully, the remaining leaves hanging limply and the mysterious darkness of the spaces in between the trees. What chills me are the shadow forms that have come out of the dark places. They look as though they're waiting for someone to join them on the riverbank. Their eyes burn with sinister invitation.

Immediately, I concentrate as I've never concentrated before but Matt's mind is closed to me. During the few times when he didn't want to communicate with me, he could never manage to hide where he was. For the first time, I have no way of knowing where my grandson is. The only sensation I receive, as I whisper his name again and again, is one of fear. My grandson is deeply afraid and can't or is being prevented from making contact with me.

Suddenly, all the things I've done and learned since dying seem frivolous, meaningless tricks and games that made me feel delighted with myself for being so clever. As of this moment, things have taken on a new dimension and I know that the games are over. Something powerful that I don't understand is at large and Matt is in terrible danger. With a sudden frisson, it occurs to me that tonight is All Hallows Eve when witches are supposed to roam abroad and ghosts slip back through temporary cracks into the world of men. It comes from the time of the Druids and is far, far older than Christianity. What would Thomas say to me if he were here? Perhaps even he can't help me against this pagan, evil magic of the Old World. I know his comforting presence is nowhere near to guide or advise. I'm left with the realisation that Matt's welfare depends on me and me alone.

Celia's just burst into the room, wild-eyed.

"I can't find him anywhere! I've called and called. He knows perfectly well not to go outside the garden without asking first."

Milo and William both get up hurriedly from the table. William does his best to calm Celia.

"Don't worry! He can't have gone far. He's probably found something that interests him. You know how involved he becomes when something catches his attention!"

"Who is Matt?" asks Milo, sensing the panic bubbling up in Celia.

"Celia's seven-year-old son," replies William, shortly as he struggles into his jacket.

"May I help you find him?"

William darts a look at him. He's thinking about turning down the offer. Then he shrugs slightly.

"I suppose you may as well. The more people looking, the quicker he'll be found. We'd better get a move on. It's beginning to get dark."

I leave them to hunt for Matt in their way. I must search for him in the best way I can. I have a feeling that I will need all the skill and imagination at my disposal.

I follow the river, using my eyes and ears and sense of smell in a way that was never possible when I was living. The river's roar is louder and angrier than before. Torn branches ride, bucking in the water. I see small animals, huddling under the gorse and clumps of dead bracken and I can smell their fear.

For a moment, I catch the scent of burning and far above the valley's head where the river falls in a long cascading ribbon of white, where the trees thin on the rocky ground, I think I glimpse the flickering light of a bonfire. I raise myself higher and float towards it but as quickly as it appeared, it's snuffed out. An acrid scent of smoke lies in the air as I search for the fugitive light that now springs up briefly on the other side of the valley. I feel that something's playing a deadly game with me – and I told Matt I didn't believe in ghosts.

A full moon breaks cover every now and then and the black shadows of trees cast a lacy pattern on the path far below me. I've worked my way down both sides of the valley, from the waterfall to the wooden bridge. The water has risen so high that the bridge almost seems to be resting on it like a barge. When I look carefully, I see that the centre section of handrail that faces downstream has broken. It's at the exact spot where Matt and I stood and watched the twigs he'd let fall as they raced towards the birch tree.

Out of the corner of my eye, I catch a movement further down the river, where the trees crowd close to the water's edge. As I draw closer, I can see the emaciated shadow shapes that I'd noticed on that evening walk with Matt – the figures I hadn't known he'd also seen because he never told me. They are crowded round the limp body of my grandchild.

Matt's lying on his side, half-hidden by two large boulders. His clothes are soaking wet and there's blood on his forehead. My grandson's eyes are closed and his face is white as frost in the moonlight.

Without stopping to think, I propel myself into the middle of the group. They scatter as I bend over him, then melt back in a trembling circle around us. My grandson's not dead, although he's deadly cold and his breathing comes in shallow sighs. I try to cover him with a cloak of warmth. I breathe over him, again and again. The shadows seem to be pushing in, smothering us.

"You won't take him! He doesn't belong in your

phantom world. Leave him and go back to where you belong," I scream at the swaying shapes pressing down on us.

There is the sound of a collective sigh, like leaves briefly stirred by an unexpected wind. Suddenly, I understand that these sad skeletal shapes are from famine times; driven from their homes, forced from their land, they fled – only to perish in the coffin ships. They bring with them the bitter odour of an ancient anger as they revisit the fallen stones of roofless cottage and barn. I realise too that they can only exercise their malign power over the few who are aware of their presence.

Because I don't know what else to do, I trace the form of a cross in the air around me and mutter the jumbled words of half-forgotten prayers. I pray to any God that will listen, to all that is good in the world and outside it and I breathe my soul into my grandson.

All night long I will keep this vigil. I will be a barrier against all the hate and despair that is trying to force itself into Matt's world and into my mind. I won't lose hope. I will stay by his side until the daylight comes.

Chapter Twenty-three

The first glimmer of dawn spreads across the sky. I am drained – so drained that I can hardly think rationally. I feel almost as if all the energy I had has left me and I've become completely transparent.

They have gone now, slipping silently back to wherever it is they belong. They haven't taken my grandson with them. As I look down at him, I realise how near to death he is. Matt's deeply unconscious, so much so that I still can't reach him. He's wandering in some strange place in his mind, far beyond my grasp. I can't tell him how much I love him and how important it is for his mother and grandfather that he comes back to them.

I have to get help quickly! Several times during the night, the others passed close to where Matt lay. It was as if the crowds of famine figures blocked us from human view with a lethal mix of shadow and freezing mists. We became invisible until first light.

William, Celia and Milo have been up all night,

searching. Now they are being helped by two gardaí. I manage to make Matt's jacket slide off his body and drape itself over the bigger of the two boulders that partially hide him. Milo is nearest to us. In desperation, I call out to him.

To my amazement, he pauses, turns his head and starts to stumble over the hummocks of wet grass towards us. I keep repeating his name so that it's ringing in his head. Nearer and nearer he comes. Suddenly he gives a shout. He's seen Matt's blue jacket. I want to weep with relief as Milo scrambles over the rocks, one of the gardaí close on his heels.

Very gently, Milo lifts my grandson and steadied by the young garda, starts the difficult journey over rocks and through brambles, up to where he can cross the wooden bridge. The jagged ends of the broken handrail show up white against the brown timber. When Celia sees Milo coming towards her, carrying Matt's limp body, she lets out a low moan.

"Oh, Matt! No!"

Milo smiles reassurance at her.

"He's alive but you need to ring for an ambulance."

Celia doesn't wait to be told twice. By the time Milo's reached the kitchen, she's rung 999 and an ambulance is on its way. Milo lays Matt on the couch and starts to strip off the child's wet clothes. Mutely, William and Celia look on. They both seem strangely paralysed.

Concentrating on what he's doing, not looking at the other two, Milo asks for blankets to wrap Matt in.

"Could you put more logs on the fire?" he asks William and my husband obediently hurries outside to fetch more logs.

239

Celia comes back with blankets and it is Milo who carefully folds them round my grandson.

"He's desperately cold. I'll rub his feet and legs. You work on his hands," he instructs Celia.

Without a murmur, she does as he tells her.

All the time they are working on Matt's body, I'm trying to get through to his mind. There is nothing there. Not a spark. Not a flicker.

While they're waiting for the ambulance to arrive, forgotten Minerva's making strange crooning noises and swaying, weaving her head backwards and forwards as though she's distressed. Finally, the welcome sound of a siren is heard, coming from the village. The youngest garda promises Celia that the squad car will accompany the ambulance as far as the main road.

A tired-looking consultant tells Celia that he's amazed Matt didn't die of hypothermia, given the coldness of the night and the length of time he had lain, soaking wet in the open air.

"He must have had his fairy godmother keeping an eye on him," he says, smiling at my pale-faced daughter. "I'm afraid she'll have her work cut out for her. We're not out of the woods yet. Your son has a couple of cracked ribs and we have to carry out a brain scan to see why he still hasn't regained consciousness."

"What will the brain scan show?" asks Celia, almost in a whisper.

"It'll give us an idea of how much brain activity there is and if there's any bleeding." Seeing the look on Celia's face, he adds, "So far, we've no reason at all to suspect there is. A child's body is a marvellous thing you know, Miss Fitzgerald. They can sleep deeply like a sick animal and then suddenly they're bouncing around, wondering what all the fuss is about."

Every day, Milo comes to the hospital to visit Matt. William and Celia seem to have accepted his presence without question. The relationship between them has changed irrevocably; the three of them are bound together after that terrible night on the mountainside. The fact that Matt is still unconscious seems to strengthen the bond.

The doctor says that nothing sinister has shown up on the scan but Celia can see that he's puzzled by the depth of Matt's coma. She sits by his bed and talks softly to him in case somewhere there is a chink in the fog of unconsciousness that will allow her voice through. She tells him that she loves him and she talks about all the things they'll do together when he's better. Somehow, she manages to keep her voice even but when she leaves the room for a break, tears spill down her cheeks and I know how terrified she is. I know because I'm frightened too. All my attempts at making contact with Matt's sleeping brain are thwarted.

William's finding this the most difficult thing he's ever had to face in his life. Exhausted, he wanders the hospital corridors and paces backwards and forwards outside the Intensive Care Unit like a caged animal. He can neither read nor write. All his energies are concentrated on the boy lying in the narrow bed. Every now and then, my husband goes to the glass screen that closes him off from his grandson. He stares at the drips and tubes attached to Matt.

He looks blankly at the monitors with their green lines that peak and fall and bleep and I hear him groping for words with which to pray. Each time he searches, he can't find the ones he needs. He's looking so old – so much more than his sixty-six years.

Milo is the strong one among them. He's tireless. He comes at different times each day, fitting his visits in between lectures. It was his idea to buy Matt a Walkman and music tapes. He's the one who gets coffee from the machine in the hall and gently insists that William sits down and drinks it while it's still hot.

Today he's propping up Celia's flagging optimism. On one of her breaks from Matt, while the nurses are busy with the tubes and plastic bags, he finds her sitting in the nearby waiting-room, head in her hands. It's been three days since Matt was brought into the hospital and she's hardly slept at all. She's afraid that if she takes pills to help her rest and Matt has some sort of crisis, she won't be in a fit state to go to him.

She looks up as Milo comes into the room.

"Hello there! How are you bearing up?" he asks gently, sitting down beside her.

"All right, I suppose." She runs her hand tiredly through her short hair. "No, not really. To be honest, I'm feeling terrible . . . and I'm so scared that Matt . . . won't get better."

Milo puts an arm around her and gives her a quick hug.

"He was always strong and healthy before this happened, wasn't he?"

"Yes, I suppose he was."

"Well, that must stand him in good stead." Milo pauses

and then asks, "Do you remember what the doctor said about how Matt must have a fairy godmother?" Celia manages a half-hearted nod. "Well, I agree with him. I felt it out on the mountainside when I found Matt and I feel it here, in this hospital. I think someone's keeping watch over him. Don't think I'm mad, but it feels like someone I know."

He looks at my daughter, anxious not to upset her by saying something she'd find too bizarre but Celia's attention is caught, so Milo decides to risk it. What he says doesn't surprise me all that much, when I think about it.

"I think your mother is here with Matt."

"My mother's dead, Milo." Celia's voice is flat.

"What do we know about death? No one's come back to tell us what goes on after we die. For what it's worth, I happen to believe that there's a benign presence watching over your son."

Celia sighs. "Well, as long as the presence is benign, I don't mind." She sits for a moment in thought and then asks, "What happened up on the mountain?"

"It was very strange. I wasn't bothering to look down near the place you call the Soldiers' Pool because I'd been there a few hours earlier and found nothing. I was concentrating higher up where the brambles and gorse come right down to the water. Suddenly, I got the weirdest feeling in my head. It sounds mad, I know but almost as if my mind was being invaded by a voice. It was a woman's and she kept saying my name, over and over again. When I went in the direction of the voice, it got louder and louder until I spotted Matt's jacket, lying on the boulder. The calling stopped immediately I saw it. The funny thing is, I'd swear blind that the jacket hadn't been there a couple of hours earlier."

Celia stares at him.

"So what you're saying is that you think the voice belonged to my mother? Do you remember how she sounded?"

"Oh, yes! Yes, I do."

Something about the way Milo says that makes Celia keep on staring at him for a few moments longer. Then, her head suddenly droops.

"I'm so tired, Milo."

He takes off his woollen scarf and folds it into a pillow.

"Curl up for a moment and have a quick nap. I'll go and watch through the glass and if there's any change, I'll come straight back and wake you, I promise."

Before he's out of the room, she's fast asleep.

Matt's coma has lasted for a whole week. The young houseman's face is serious as he talks to Celia.

"I'm afraid Matt's developed pneumonia and he's not responding to the antibiotics as he should. So, we're going to try him on some stronger ones. Hopefully, they'll deal with the infection."

He rushes off to see another patient, leaving my daughter stranded in the middle of the corridor, feeling even more frightened and hopeless than before. She has begun to loathe the sounds and smells of this alien place but knows that she has to trust her son to the white-coated, fatigued doctors and the brisk nurses who don't really have the time to talk to you. Who else can help him?

It turns out that Celia has every reason to be frightened.

Tonight Matt's temperature suddenly rockets and his breathing becomes laboured. All at once, the screens stop their even bleeping and bells and buzzers start to ring. The resuscitation trolley is called for and the young doctor appears, running down the corridor as he struggles into his white coat.

Oh, no, Matt! You can't do this to us all. I won't let you! I have a horrible feeling of déjà vu. Matt's room is on the floor immediately below the room where I died just seven weeks ago.

Suddenly, I hear his voice and there in front of me is Matt, a thin, frail wraith-like figure rising slowly from the body on the bed below. He holds out his arms to me.

"*Grand-mère Kate!* I'm coming to be with you."

He's smiling.

"No, Matt! No! You *must* go back. You can't leave your mother and grandpapa. They need you to be with them."

"But I want to be with you, *Grand-mère Kate*. We shall have such fun together!" he pleads.

For one brief moment, I hold him in my arms. I force myself to speak in a steady voice.

"Matt, darling. If you don't go back, your grandfather will die of a broken heart. Even though he will never say it, he loves you dearly. Your mother has suffered a lot because of becoming a mother to you when she was still so young. Do you want to make her unhappy for the rest of her life? No, Matt! You will go back – and quickly – before it's too late."

I release him and descend with him so that he's positioned just above himself on the bed.

"Please go back now, Matt. Do it for me as well as for the others."

"*D'accord, Grand-mère Kate,*" he says, with a regretful smile. "After all, I suppose I have many words still to teach to Minerva. *Adieu!*"

The Matt who nearly became like me slips back into his other self, as easily as sliding a hand into a glove – and is gone.

The green lines on the monitors have resumed their bleeps.

"Thank God for that! He's back with us," someone says, in a tired voice.

I can feel myself trembling all over.

Chapter Twenty-four

He still looks frail, but Matt is on the mend. He's been moved out of Intensive Care and is now in the children's ward. Celia spends a large part of each day sitting by his bed, reading to him, holding and hugging him – when he'll let her – his ribs are very sore. She keeps looking at him as though she can't believe he's really there.

Matt's hoping that Milo will appear soon. Since my grandson regained consciousness three days ago, the two of them have built up a strong friendship. Before Milo said anything, Matt seemed to know that the topic of *Grand-mère Kate* was not out of bounds. He recognises the Milo he once spotted in my thoughts. When Celia and William are not around, Matt talks to him about me.

When Milo sticks his head round the door to the ward, my grandson's face lights up. Celia goes to have a cup of coffee and he takes her place at Matt's bedside.

I've not tried to see into his thoughts – but I'm pretty sure that he's been thinking of me a lot recently. Yesterday, he spoke out loud, as he was sitting in his car in the hospital car park.

"If you can hear me, Kate. I want you to know that I never stopped loving you and that time we had together remains one of my happiest memories. But I'm not going to grieve for you because I know that you weren't happy when you were alive. I just hope that, wherever you are, you're happy now. I don't know why, but something tells me you had a hand in Matt's recovery. He's a great kid. He really is. Thank you."

Then he just sat there quietly for a while with his eyes closed.

He's put off asking Matt too many questions but I know he can't hold off any longer. As soon as Celia's gone he puts his elbows on the bed, leans forward, resting his chin on clasped hands and looks Matt straight in the eye.

"Tell me what happened on the mountain, Matt."

But Matt won't talk about Hallowe'en night.

"I can't remember – only that *Grand-mère Kate* was with me."

"What did she do?"

"She helped me," is all he will say. To make up for his stubbornness, he suddenly asks, "Milo, do you remember when all the machines started making funny noises and the green lines went flat?"

"Your poor mother told me about it, yes."

"Well, I went to see *Grand-mère Kate*. We talked together!"

Milo gives him a funny look and then says, "You talked with your grandmother?"

"Yes, I really did. I was a ghost too – I floated – just like her."

Milo's silent for a moment while he digests this piece of information.

"What did she say to you?"

"She said that I must go back quickly to Mama and Grandpapa. She said they needed me and if I didn't go back, they would be very sad." He shrugs. "So I came back!"

"It sounds to me as though you've had an out-of-body experience, Matt. Could you feel yourself leaving and rejoining your body?" asks Milo, fascinated.

"Oh, yes!" Matt searches for the most vividly accurate way to describe the experience. "It was like being – a sausage sliding out of its skin – or a snake. It was great!"

Milo laughs.

"I don't think any of *us* would use that precise word to describe what happened. I'm glad you decided to come back to us though – after all that excitement." He suddenly looks serious. "Matt, how did your grandmother look?"

Matt seems surprised by the question.

"She looked OK. She was nice but a little sad, perhaps. I think she was worried about me."

Matt hesitates and then asks, "Could you . . . touch her?"

"Not like if she was properly alive but she put her arms around me and I could feel something." Matt's searching for the right words. "I felt suddenly warm and I'd been cold for a long time – and she made me feel safe." He looks at Milo to see if he understands.

There is a pause before Milo says, "I think you're very lucky to have a grandmother like that, don't you?"

"Yes," says my grandson, nodding vehemently.

Bless him!

After all the panic over Matt, I'm feeling rather . . . diminished. I wouldn't want to have to go through more of the same! This past week has taken a lot out of everyone, especially William; he's looking completely washed out but he's so full of relief that he hasn't noticed yet how tired he is.

Everything seems to be sorting itself out, though: Matt's on the mend and now Veronica's rung William.

"William! Celia's just told me about Matt. I'm so sorry! You must have been desperately worried. Why didn't you let me know what had happened?"

She sounds hurt. I just hope that my husband isn't going to make a mess of this. Be careful, William, please!

"Well, to be honest, none of us were thinking straight while Matt was first of all missing and then so ill . . . There was a time when we thought he wasn't going to make it . . . Also, I wasn't sure you'd want me getting in touch after our last meeting."

"Do you feel any differently since then?"

"I know that I miss you, Veronica."

"Would you like me to come out at the weekend – just for a little while?"

"Yes, please do. That would be nice."

William sounds so formal – but that's just his way. Veronica must love him – she obviously hasn't given up on him.

Then there's Celia and Milo. They've started the slow, sweet process of falling in love but they don't know it yet. It's strange to see the man who was, for a short time, my lover, gazing thoughtfully at my daughter when she doesn't know he's looking.

During the time Matt was ill, Milo wanted to do

anything he could to ease the burden from Celia. He found her wild-eyed and sometimes out-of-control distress, gut-wrenching. He was moved too by William's stoicism; how the man could hardly bear to look at his grandson's inert body on the hospital bed and how he too struggled for ways to comfort Celia. Milo watched as William was reduced to hours of silent pacing along the hospital corridors when the tension and anxiety became too much for him and he felt like an impotent bystander in the drama unfolding around him.

Celia's too wrapped up in Matt to realise that she's attracted to Milo. I think at the moment, if she were to be asked about him, she would acknowledge how supportive he's been and say that he's a nice man. And he *is* a nice man. Seeing him again has brought back so many happy memories of our short time together. I hope my daughter allows him into her life. She can be so busy being headstrong, she gets blinded to what's really happening around her sometimes.

I think that William and Milo will keep secret the time Milo and I loved each other. It will be relegated to the past – where it belongs. It's clear that Milo and Matt like each other – perhaps that will help her see the light!

I would like to know that she'll be happy before I have to leave them all. Thomas's words keep ringing in my ears and I get the feeling that I haven't much time left.

Minerva's jumping around her cage like a parrot half her age because Matt has come home. Celia helps him in the door on his wobbly legs. The first thing he asks for is a chair so that he can sit beside the parrot and have a talk.

As soon as he sits down, Minerva gives him the two-step, head-bobbing greeting, then launches into her favourite song about the drunken sailor. Matt joins in, laughing.

William and Celia watch them from the other side of the room.

"It's so good to have him home again," says my husband. Then he hurriedly adds, "And you too, of course."

Celia suddenly stands on tiptoe and gives him a quick kiss on the cheek.

"Thanks, Dad. Thanks for everything."

"That's the trouble; I didn't *do* anything," William says. "I just watched you being put through the mill. I think I was pretty useless really. It was the same when you were small. Your mother did all the caring and cherishing and more than her share of worrying."

Celia shakes her head vehemently.

"No! That's just where you're wrong. You were there all the time and you cared. That's what mattered."

"Yes, well. I'm just going into my study for a little while." At the door, William turns. Casually, he says, "Oh, by the way, Veronica might be dropping in at the weekend."

Equally casually, Celia replies, "Good. That'll be nice."

It's dark now as I wait for Thomas to come. All my instincts tell me that he will be here soon. I'm floating above the house in the Red Glen, where I lived for nearly thirty years. I've revisited all its corners and passed from room to room, remembering.

I hope that some slight trace of me will remain, for a while at least. I would like to think that the loving, positive thoughts I have as I say goodbye to my home, will linger on and perhaps even have some sort of beneficial influence on the lives that will be lived out there.

Milo's been invited for supper with William, Celia and Matt. This means that all the people I care about most in the world are sharing a meal together under the same roof.

Veronica's coming out tomorrow. I was so angry with her when I first learned the truth about her and William. Now, I'm just glad that she hasn't turned her back on him and that my tempestuous daughter's realised, before it was too late, that it would be no bad thing if her father and Veronica can be together for at least some of the time. I've no illusions about them living cosily together in married bliss. They're both too set in their ways for that – and Veronica's horrible cat would probably eat Minerva – if Minerva didn't eat the cat first.

I hope that if Celia and Milo get together, they will manage things better than William and I did. I have a feeling they will. Celia so needs loving and Milo has great armfuls of love and tenderness to give.

And Matt! He's the hardest of all to leave. I can't go without saying goodbye. So, I wait until he's gone to bed and is alone for the first time this evening.

I slowly make my way down to earth for my last visit.

He looks up as soon as I come into the room.

"Hello, *Grand-mère Kate!*" With his usual quickness, he knows at once that something's different. "What is the matter? Why are you looking like that?"

"Nothing's the matter, Matt. Nothing at all! It's just that the time's come when I have to say goodbye to you."

Poor Matt! He wasn't expecting this. He sits bolt upright in bed, his mouth open like a small fish out of water.

"*Non! Ce n'est pas possible!* I don't want you to go. You belong here with me and Minerva."

"No, my dear. I think I was only allowed to stay while I tried to get you all together. Now you are a proper family and it's time for me to go. After all, no one wants a dead granny hanging around the place for the rest of their lives, do they?"

His eyes fill with tears.

"I thought you would always stay. Where will you go?"

"That's what I have to find out now. Just remember how happy I am to have known my grandson and how proud I am of him. Tell Milo that I love you all. Will you do that for me, Matt?" He nods, unable to speak. He looks so miserable. I move close to him. I want you to do something else for me too. I want you to lie down and close your eyes and not be sad."

Eventually he lies down and tries to do what I asked. After a few seconds, his eyelids flicker open.

"I'm still sad inside," he says, in a small voice.

Finally he sleeps.

I move close to his ear and whisper, "Matt, you'll forget everything that happened that night on the mountain. You'll lose the ability you had to see things other people couldn't and you'll only remember me as a dream – not as a ghost. In this way, you won't ever be at the mercy of the others out there who might do you harm. Goodbye, my dearest Matt. Sleep peacefully."

I rise from the house like a gust of wind, not looking back.

Thomas is there, waiting, as I knew he would be.

For the first time I see him as he truly is and I am nearly

blinded by the terrible beauty of his face. He shines with an incandescent light that is almost unbearable. My Guardian Angel holds out his hand.

"Are you ready, Kate?"

I take a deep breath.

"Yes," I say. "As ready as I'll ever be."

The End